the dog

By

david paul kirkpatrick
&
steven james taylor

Illustrations by
steven james taylor

Happiness  Publishing

the dog
by david paul kirkpatrick and steven james taylor
© Copyright 2018 by ARX LLC. All rights reserved.

Happiness Publishing
Box 445
Sturbridge, MA 01566

Illustrations by steven james taylor
Cover and design by Lewis Design & Marketing
ISBN: 978-1-943785-85-8
10 9 8 7 6 5 4 3 2 1

1. Fiction - Action and Adventure 2. Adult Fiction
Printed in U.S.A.

For our moms,
Jean and Sandra Jean

Just ask the animals, and they will teach you.
Ask the birds of the sky, and they will tell you.
Speak to the earth, and it will instruct you.
Let the fish in the sea speak to you.

— Job 12:7–8 (NLT)

ii

Note on Typography

Ted Snow suffered from a learning disability, largely un-treated in the era of his life. In honor of Ted's story and in respect for all those who struggle with reading, we have used the Nova Lineta ITC font. The font has a great deal of air in it, making it especially easy to read. From experience, we have found the font to be helpful with those challenged by dyslexia. It was designed by Slobodan Jelesijev who specializes in spatial graphics at the University of Nis.

Acknowledgments

We are grateful to the dogs who have contributed to this work. They include, in no particular order: Coffee, Arthur, Leo, Jake, Shadow (the original wolf-dog of Cape Cod), Bathsheba, Maximillian, Benjamin, Heather, and Hudson. Of course, there are many more: the neighbors' dogs, the dogs of the street, and the dogs that have graced our TV and movie screens.

We thank all those who have not only thought about dogs but written about them: Henry David Thoreau, Walt Whitman, Robert Frost, Rudyard Kipling, Pablo Neruda, John Homans, John Steinbeck, and perhaps, most importantly, Mary Oliver. We have listened on audio to Mary Oliver's beautiful and touching collections that she reads herself, *Dog Songs* and *A Thousand Mornings*, more than we can count.

Writing something together is a challenge, so we are grateful for the times we could be in the same physical space at the same time. But we must also thank the internet mother and all her children: Microsoft, Apple, Dropbox, and Box.

There would be no acknowledgements for there wouldn't have been a book without the encouragement and understanding of our friends and family: Caitlin Taylor, Sandra Jean Taylor, Matthew Taylor, Jean Zyskowski, Miroslav Jamina, Sifu Cruz, Dado, Josh, Brendon, Ellen, Arthur and Mary-Kate, and Weyland. We thank Trudy Ramirez and Craig Boone for their insights on the early drafts. We are grateful for Haley Hampton, our editor, for slogging through the many manuscripts and breathing into the work with her exceptional ideas.

This is a story of dogs, but it is also a story of America, of creative destruction: of the death of the patriarchy and the rise of a more balanced reign of male and female energies. We are Americans who still believe in the American experiment. This is a story written, edited, printed, and published by Americans in America. We are thankful for our Chicago-based publishers, Rabbit; our printers, Bang, located in Brainerd, Minnesota; and our distributors, Anchor, in New Kensington, Pennsylvania, and Diamond, who bring not only Superman and the Walking Dead to the world from their Baltimore-based headquarters, but now, this dog.

We thank the women who helped us try to get right the nuance and detail in our fashioning of America's indigenous tribes: Paula Peters and Lindsay A. Randall. Through them, we now have an even deeper respect for the men and women who came before us on these American shores.

We want to thank our partners at NEADS, who steadfastly support and train World Class Service Dogs and match them with individuals with disabilities. We especially wish to thank Cathy Zemaitis, Gerry DeRouche, Doreen Sheridan, and Audrey Trieschman for their help. We love how dogs are elevated in their sphere. Our world needs more NEADS.

We have only gratitude for the good folks at the Emily Dickinson Museum in Amherst, Massachusetts. Because of them, we were able to spend time in the "Mighty Room" in preparation for the final manuscript. Like so many others, we experienced the muse of the room while we worked.

Lastly, we wish to thank you for picking up this book and for not yet assuming that you have read the last word on the mystery and magic of the dog. We hope and pray that this book brings you to a deeper understanding not only of our furry friends, but of Nature with a capital N.

Prologue

In the back right corner of the top drawer, Theo Snow stashed the important stuff. He had always done that. He could not remember why. Past his socks, a broken wristwatch, and his mismatched cuff-links, there it was—fragrant from a spilled bottle of aftershave—the small memory heap of his life. In the seemingly random pile were love letters, baseball cards, a few graduation diplomas, and washed-out warranties.

While he was only twenty-nine, there was much Theo could not remember. But he could recall the exact hiding place of the photo he searched for. The photo was smoothed inside a crumbling Christmas card envelope from his great-aunt Mary. He found the old envelope, gummy from the stickers of red-and-green elves and cartoon reindeer. Then he crammed the other stuff back into the corner of the drawer. With finality, he shut the bureau.

Death is a door.

For those of us left living, once the door is closed, it is easy to grow bewildered by loss and the ephemerals. But Theo Snow did not want to become undone. Not now. He wanted to stay tethered to where he was through memory. In this present sorrow, it would be the right thing to do. Death was a door. But that bureau drawer was a window into remembrance. A door closes. A window opens. Life turns. Isn't that the way the music of the spheres plays?

What did New England poet Robert Frost say? "In three words I can sum up everything I've learned about life—it goes on."

Chapter One

The storm arrived without warning. Rain lashed against the walls of the house. The thunder grumbled, shaking the dormers of the bedroom. Like machine-gun bullets, the wind-driven raindrops *rat-a-tat-tatted* against the window panes. Theo's mind glimmered in the cold-blue convulsions of the tumultuous night.

He watched the forks of lightning flash onto the faces of the hundred Supermans surrounding his bed, their red capes bared, ready to defend cause or country. But the sentient eyes of the Supermans stayed staunch, anchored in pasted paper upon the four walls. These heroes to American boys did not leap, despite their bodies standing strong in their paper capes.

Frightened to his core, his insides liquid with panic, Theo Snow hugged his pillow. Sometimes, the safest place to be was inside the eye of the storm. Still, the comfort in his small bed made Theo feel tragic, his mattress a coffin, the bludgeoning rain his burial soil.

When he heard the shout in the squall, blood rushed into his ears. Nauseated, ears pulsing, Theo leapt from his bed, ripping himself from his uneasy comfort. The shout came from his mother.

He knew the shout only too well.

In his bare feet, he skittered across the wooden floor to the door, throwing it open against the storm, crashing it wide to the hallway. As he sailed into the corridor, he saw a monstrous dragoon upon his mother, oppressing her with wild unrest.

"No, Theo!" Alice Snow shouted. "Back into your room!"

She tumbled forward to the door, reaching him, pushing him back from the blurred, capsizing hallway, away from the large typhoon-hands gusting across her body. Dumb with shock, Theo watched as his mother yanked on the white porcelain knob and slammed the door shut.

"Stay there!" she shouted from the other side of the door. Her screams grew muffled.

Theo did not know what to do but kneel at the side of the bed and pray to whoever or whatever might be out there to protect his mother. As he looked up through his prayer fingers, he saw the fleet of Supermans, row after row.

Can't you get us out of this?

No fury can last forever. It will always play itself out. Such is the mystery of wind. So it was with this storm. Gusts died with the breaking clouds. Shouts softened to laments. The machine-gun fire melted into gently falling rain. As it was the middle of the night, larks did not herald the morning. Instead, quietude swelled across the dreadful winter sky.

Theo felt the breath of his mother above him.

"Is it alright if I stay in here tonight?" she asked. Her breath smelled of fresh blood and Wrigley's Juicy Fruit.

He looked up from his sleep and saw his mother's swollen cheek. Her green lioness eyes pooled with tears. He nodded yes.

He opened his covers for her.

"Oh, you're too big for that. I brought a blanket and a pillow," she answered. With her things, she lay down on the round hooked rug.

"Why don't we switch, Mom?" asked Theo. He put on his tortoise-shell eyeglasses from the night table. He peered over the side of his bed, glimpsing Alice on the floor, her auburn hair in a stormy aftermath about her head.

"Oh, sweetie, I am already comfy here," she replied, as she pushed her hair back and looked at him with crushed eyes. And it seemed to Theo that she was already dreaming as she spoke to him, the attention of her gaze already gone from her shaken body, sleep her true escape. Even at the age of eleven, Theo knew much. Whatever the attitude of his mother's body, he understood that her soul was on its knees.

He returned to his pillow but could not sleep.

The branches of the sweetgum tree in the yard scraped at his window.

The white porcelain knob turned on the wooden door.

The storm pushed on the wood, again.

It could not gain entrance without force. Then as Theo heard the foot falls of the storm retreat, the principality of sky fell across the farmhouse like a mystic veil of forgetting.

A white-breasted robin with a yellow bill warbled from the

sweetgum tree. The kitchen smelled of coffee and warming toast. When Theo entered the kitchen the following morning, his mother was already whisking the eggs. As he observed the face powder on the side of his mother's cheek, the ruin of the cold-blue night raced across his mind.

"Are you okay, Mom?" he asked as he made his way to the stove. There she poured the eggs into the fry pan. They sizzled. He reached up. She leaned down.

"I'm fine," Alice answered as she kissed him on the forehead. "About last night. You know, your father went out with his friends. They just returned from France. They were out celebrating."

"Celebrating?" Theo asked as he sat down at the kitchen table. He was furious. He was always furious after the storm—furious with himself for being incapable of defending his mom. "Is that what you call it?"

"The war's over, Theo. Our troops are returning. It is a great time to be alive! Why shouldn't there be celebrations?"

Alice, who had been avoiding looking at her son, turned. More than ever, Theo could see the bloated damage beneath the thin, rosy mask of her makeup.

"He feels bad, Theo, about the medical discharge."

"Having bad eyes is not his fault, Mom," Theo replied, pushing his own glasses up the bridge of his young Roman nose.

"And seeing his friends last night," Alice continued. "Well, I suppose he felt less of a man."

"So, by hitting you, now he's more of one?"

"He didn't hit me, Theo. It was the alcohol."

"So, it was the alcohol that hit your face, not his fist?"

In reply to Theo's question, Alice's mouth closed. Her face grew grim and New England stoic. In his defense, Theo was not trying to be a smart aleck. He was being a dutiful son who loved his mom, who yearned to come to her aid. He was a Boy Scout, after all. He had already climbed from Scout to Tenderfoot. Someday, he might be an Eagle.

Ted Snow came into the tidy, cool, scrubbed kitchen. He wore a short-sleeve shirt that revealed arms knotted with awkward country muscles. His dungarees still held the store-bought blue of a recent purchase from Montgomery Ward. In the hot winter light, the yellow skin of his face looked sickly. At eight in the morning, his prescription sunglasses were already hiding his eyes.

"Morning, champ," Ted said as he tousled Theo's hair with his fleshy hand. Theo could smell him. Hercules smelled of freshly ironed clothes. He walked cheerfully across the kitchen and kissed Alice on the cheek. "Morning, Mother."

"Why do you call her 'mother'?" Theo snapped, trying to restrain his insolence.

"No, suh," replied the man, absently.

"She is your wife!"

"Yuh, she is all that, but can you mind your own business, champ?"

"My name is not champ. My name is Theo!"

"No, suh."

Ted smiled as he looked back at his son. He lowered his sunglasses to reveal disinterested eyes staring from inside puffy rings of flesh. He pushed the green lenses over his eyes and grabbed the doorknob to leave.

"I'll be back tonight, sweetheart. Seeing the guys this

morning for breakfast at the Windjammer."

"But, Ted, you saw them last night," Alice replied.

"Yuh. I haven't seen them in two years, honey. We have a lot of catching up to do." He walked out, closing the door behind him. It squeaked its damning squeak.

"I still think it's creepy that he calls you 'mother,'" Theo said.

"Why wouldn't he call me 'mother'?" Alice asked with a hint of happy mischief. By changing her tone, she instantly trans-formed the atmosphere of the kitchen. Theo thought his mom was magic. "I am the mother of the greatest boy on earth."

It would have been easy for Theo to grow ironic. He could walk through life with a paradoxical chip on his shoulder, with skin like armor. But Alice did not want to raise a boy who looked at life askew. Alice wanted her son to greet the day with elation. She wanted to raise her boy into a wholesome man.

"The greatest boy? Not by a long shot, Mom," replied Theo. With energy, Alice Snow came to the table and sat her thin, lithe body next to her son.

"And do you know what the greatest boy on earth should have?"

"I have no idea since I am not the greatest boy."

"A dog."

"You're kidding."

"No, I am not kidding."

"A real dog? Not an oil-painting dog or a stuffed-animal dog?"

"No, I mean a real-live dog," she replied, laughing. "A dog you can fetch with and run to the marshes with."

Theo was breathless.

He darted up from his chair. Alice's thin, angular arms were made of tenderness, always there for Theo. He hugged her, letting go, for a moment, of his awful terror.

"Hurry, Theo, the bus will be here."

Theo grabbed his jacket and rucksack from the hook in the mud room.

"When?" he asked.

"As soon as we can find the right one," she replied. "It's spring soon enough. Spring always brings its share of puppies."

Smiling, he raced out the kitchen door. The cursed door squeaked its damnation.

Of course, for an eleven-year-old boy, soon could not come fast enough. On the school bus, which smelled of gas and freshly sharpened pencils, Theo asked everyone for information about any known litter of puppies.

No one had heard of any.

In his sixth-grade class, Theo made a special announcement to anyone who knew of an available dog. His classmates were of the melting pot—the sons and daughters of hard-working people. Of immigrants—of the Irish, the English, the Portuguese. Of workers—fishermen, builders, farmers, and seamstresses. Of the first born—the Native Americans. His classmates did not know of any new puppies. Theo could not understand where the dogs were.

It was spring, after all.

The rain bore the snow and ice away. In November, the

rams and ewes had mated. Now, in April, the black-faced lambs gamboled from the wintering barns into the tender grasses. Worms inched across oozing mud. Woodpeckers knocked against softening bark. Birds filled the warming sky with clouds of song.

Theo knew his mom was right. Spring was a perfect time for puppies, and Theo, well, Theo was going to find one by the sheer force of his will. The boy was brash, arrogant, and feisty. He was as young as the teeming spring. He did not yet have the eyes of a traveler who saw the world through his soul. He was still a tourist who arrived at a place, seeing with his eyes.

What Theo could not glimpse was the expanding universe already turning under the power of his mother's intention. All of us are capable of such force if only we understood how to wield it. She had already prayed for his dog. Her rhythm, that attitude that could change the atmosphere of any room, was already rippling the air. The puppy was already leaping forward, discovering him. Theo was only eleven. He did not yet know the elemental law of life—every rhythm prepares a future.

CHAPTER TWO

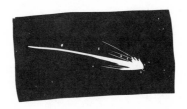

A silver star hurled across the black sky, falling through the inky air of Pleasant Bay. It seemed to tumble at the feet of Ahanu Lightstone. The tall, strapping man stood on the paved tar of the Monomoy Gas Station and stared. Ahanu had finished servicing a 1945 Chevrolet sport sedan. Its green fins had just swum free of the pump bathed in the purple neon of the station sign.

Ahanu's face was tough, weather-scarred, as timeless as a figurehead on an old ship might be. But the eyes twinkled in the hard face. To Ahanu, the comet was a sign of change. As a medicine man for his tribe who spoke the ancient Algonquin language, Ahanu descended from the first world. In that world, man's knowingness was not merely in the mind, but in the tree, the ocean, and the stars. Man spoke for Nature. And Nature spoke for Man. As Ahanu looked at the shooting star, something fresh entered his life, for the silver rip in the darkness opened a door of new adventure for his spirit.

As he looked up from the station at the sky, a flatbed truck with Louisiana plates rolled onto the tar. He had been waiting for it. The three cars on the truck were hardly new. They were being delivered for engine removal and parting. The war in Europe had made auto parts in the States sparse. This part of New England always needed electrical components, switches, and starters to keep the wheels of small businesses humming.

Ahanu told the driver to grab some coffee and a sandwich inside the station and take a load off. The driver was grateful. Ahanu and his men drove the truck to the back and unloaded the cars.

Later, Ahanu locked the cash register, turned the main lights off, and secured the office to the Monomoy Station. Ahanu means he who laughs. He laughed easily as a child, but tonight he was gripped by grandeur. His countenance was deadly serious as he walked to the back of the garage to lock the gate to the salvage yard where the three cars rested.

The falling star stretched his human senses. He felt the spring corn growing in the distant field. He smelled the drops of tomorrow's rain. The night was quiet. He would take the stairs to the second-floor apartment of the station where he lived with his wife, Oota Dabun, named after a star that shined in the day. Ahanu was hungry. Oota Dabun had made a chicken stew with the early greens of the season.

As he headed to lock the gate, Ahanu heard a whining near the delivered cars. He walked through the gate to investigate the salvage further. It might be a fox sniffing out some food left in one of the trunks. When startled, foxes could be vicious.

He picked up a rake for prodding or protecting himself. He wasn't quite sure which.

The rusting trunk of the cyan-blue Cabriolet carried a large structural dent. The whine emanated from inside. He stamped the tin comb of the rake against the locked trunk.

It sounded dense with weight . . . or life. Again, he wasn't quite sure which. Ahanu returned to the edge of the station and poured water from a spigot into a small clean pan. Returning to the yard, he fixed the pan beneath the back tire of the Cabriolet. Flipping a nearby lawn chair, he sat down.

"Okay," he said, "you got in there." He folded his arms to wait. "Let's see you get out." As a trained medicine man, Ahanu had spent much time waiting for Nature. Because a shooting star had fallen at his boots, he was going to wait. And wait he did.

"Honey," called Oota Dabun. She stood on the second story porch that led to the outdoor stairs. "Dinner's ready."

"Turn down the burner and come here," he said.

"Why?" she laughed. "Is that you sitting in the salvage yard?"

"It is. We have a stowaway," he said. His eyes caught her eyes. His voice was timbered. Rich with age. Grinning, Oota Dabun returned to the kitchen, turned off the stove, and climbed down the exterior flight of wooden stairs.

"Friendly?" she asked as she stood at the gate to the salvage yard.

"Not sure," he said. "But let's wait a minute. The water should draw the *animosh* out." He opened his arms softly to her. "Come on in. There's room." His lilt was playful, romantic. Oota Dabun came to him. He drew her into his lap.

Her brow was streaked with a dozen folds from her hard-fought life. The skin about her eyes was laced with a hundred tiny crimps. Her silver hair was pulled back from her face and tied at the neck. Her violet eyes shined from her nut-brown face. Oota Dabun was as timeless and as beautiful as her husband.

She sat on his lap on the green-and-yellow lawn chair. She gazed out at the dumpy cars. "The adventures we go on," she said with a sigh. He laughed. He nuzzled her neck sweetly.

"Oh, Oota, hadn't you heard?" he said with a smile. "Our adventuring days are through."

"Ha," she replied, laughing.

"Well, I did see a shooting star. It seemed to fall at my boots."

"Aha. But then what, Ahanu," she asked knowingly, "doesn't fall at your boots?"

He laughed. She laughed again. After a few minutes, there came a soft sound from the crushed side panel of the Cabriolet. A scrawny golden dog, boney and of medium size, squeezed out of the rusted panel and beneath the wheel. Flakes of rust fell. The raggedy dog leaned into the bucket and, drinking, stayed there until the water was gone. The Lightstones watched, mesmerized, not wanting to disturb the animal.

The dog, a she, raised her head and observed the couple staring at her. She had pebbled markings of gold about her face. Her chest and haunches bore rows of black and gold, like a starved Bengal tiger. She made no overtures to the couple. She loped back to her den. Even in her wretchedness, she carried herself with dignity. As her limp and golden tail disappeared, Ahanu heard the tiny, suckling sounds from under the trunk. The voices were small and high.

The reason for her noble countenance was now clear.

She was a mother.

"Oh, there are puppies," he said. He moved to stand. Oota Dabun put her hand on his knee to stop him.

She, too, was a mother. "Nothing to do yet," she said. "I'll boil some bone broth for her while we eat. You'll bring her some chicken and rice. It will be the right thing for her intestines. Let's give her a night to get settled and nourished," she said.

As he gazed upon his wife, Ahanu was filled with a love that felt larger than both of them. Tonight, Oota Dabun embodied the sweet reassurance of maternal radiance. He was humbled by the depth of his feelings for her.

"I need to pay attention tonight," Ahanu said. A candle sparkled in an earthen plate. He sat back from his chair at the dinner table. He complimented his wife on the hot bread and stew.

"When I saw the shooting star, I sensed a . . . a yearning."

"Yearning for what?" Oota Dabun asked softly.

"I don't know for certain. It was the pain of a stranger. Lost. Needing a guide."

"But who, then? Can you see a face?" she asked.

"I do not know . . . but I know it is tied to those dogs. There's something . . ." he said.

"And what is the something?" she asked.

"It is not clear," he answered. "We shall pray."

Holding hands across the table, they beseeched the Great Spirit.

Gitche Manitou, give us the hearts to understand.

From their prayer fingers, a magic mist rose. As the vapor ascended, it caught the light of the candle. The music of the spheres opened to the light of a ghost. Pinched eyes rolled in the apparition's troubled face as she lifted into the air above the dinner table. The specter opened her pale womb. She pulled a howling, reddened child from the mist. The mother and child were the beings we have come to know as Alice and Theo Snow.

The mother beseeched her Lord to help her young son. She wanted him to grow whole. She knew only too well that rage could destroy the spirit. She was worried about her husband's anger. And her son was full of fury. She had only one weapon—to pray a new dream of living.

Later, Ahanu, too tall and wide for his leather jacket, brought bone broth and a great bucket of cut, baked chicken and rice to the blue Cabriolet. Ahanu was almost delicate, maternal, in his handling of the two buckets as he fixed them beneath the tire hub.

He watched as the mother, smelling the warm sustenance, slowly emerged from the crushed panel. The queen of black-and-golden fur not only ate, but she luxuriated in the warm bone broth. She lapped every drop of it. She chewed the chicken and rice as if breathing in fragrance, effortlessly, and as if in one long intake. Then, in some kind of ritual, she lay on her back. Excitedly, she ground her spine into the ground. On her back, she was taking the scent of this warm nourishment back to her children.

In the morning, Oota Dabun pulled a crowbar from the shed and opened the trunk of the Cabriolet. In the trunk, there was one live mother, two dead babies, and seven alive, but sickly, boys. The youngsters appeared to be but a few days old. Their eyes were still half-closed. Oota Dabun took the filthy mother into her hands and warmed her. Frail and under-nourished, the mother's ribs pierced her matted coat. Still, Oota Dabun, a mother and grandmother many times over, held the dog as if to give the vitality of her own bones and blood to her.

With help from the men at the station, Oota Dabun moved

the surviving pups and the mother to the wintering barn. Most of the horses and cows had been moved into the pastures for summer so there was lots of room.

Oota Dabun gave the golden mother a stable of her own. She lay fresh straw down and then a woolen blanket. Then, the men buried the dead infants in the soil by a fencepost on the Christmas tree farm. The trees were part of Ahanu's property.

Oota Dabun continued to feed the weak mother. She brought a chicken from the coop to the chopping block. She kissed the hen's beak in gratitude, knowing the hen would nourish many youngsters through her sacrifice.

After the blessing, Oota Dabun took an ax to the hen's neck. The death was instant. Painless. Such is the mercy that comes from the slayer who knows one day he or she shall also be slain. She plucked and baked the chicken, which produced more bone broth and more meat for the mother and her seven youngsters.

In but a few days, the boys had become lusty nurslings. The mother put on weight. The boys opened their eyes, awakening to the bright life around them.

By the third week, the puppies were walking, swatting playfully at each other with their paws, and wrestling in the dry warmth of the stable. They yipped and yapped. Expressing themselves. Trying out their voices.

With their rowed markings of brown, black, and gold, like sun and shadow, like their mother, they looked more like Bengal tiger cubs than New England mutts. As for Ahanu and Oota Dabun, they delighted in the recovery of the once-weakened mother and her hardy litter of pups.

Dr. John Cook, a veterinarian for the county's large animals, was one of Monomoy Station's regular customers. At the direction of Ahanu, Dr. Cook made a visit to the wintering barn. For Cook, as he stared through his thick, round glasses, the pups all appeared healthy, but the mother battled a low-grade infection, palpable in her eyes. The vet prescribed her a cycle of medicine for fourteen days.

"There's a mother on Blueberry Farm looking for a dog for her boy," said Dr. Cook.

Ahanu perked up at the mention. When the doctor spoke, the modernism of Ahanu's America faded from view. For him, Gitche Manitou stirred not only the rain, but the heart's inner room. Ahanu had seen the wraith of the mother crying out to him above the kitchen table. By experiencing such a stirring from Dr. Cook's conversation, Ahanu understood that he must bend toward the doctor.

"Oh?" Ahanu said. His timbered voice lifted in curiosity.

Ahanu held up the smallest nursling for the doctor to view. He had a blonde-brown coat and large, dark eyes. His yellow ears flopped over his ear canals, making his tri-colored head look as round as a harvest moon. A white line ran up his little brow and exploded in a splash of white at his crown. "He's my shooting star." Ahanu rubbed the furry white star with the pad of his thumb. "I saw him fly through the sky the night we found the mother. He is meant for greatness!"

"The runt?" said Dr. Cook, laughing.

"Oh, don't be such a Puritan, Dr. John. Have you no sense of romance?" asked Ahanu as he exploded in laughter.

"Just calling it as I see it," said the doctor with a smile.

"He happens to be the strong one." The willful puppy wig-gled in Ahanu's hands. He lapped his tiny, rough tongue on his fingers. "He has had to fight for everything from his bigger brothers! And he has been waiting for this boy of whom you tell."

"You mean he's the only one left?" said the vet with a smile. Despite the prejudices, the Lightstones were loved by many in their community. The asks for the dogs had come quickly. As the boy on the blueberry farm knew only too well, there were very few new dogs that particular spring.

"Because I have been saving him for just the right child!" Ahanu said as he held the three-week-old puppy up to his face and nuzzled him. "The boy's mother wants a friend for her son. A friend wrapped in Nature."

"Can I take a picture?" asked the doctor. "To show to the mother . . . er . . . just in case she doesn't quite buy the flying-through-the-sky bit? She is a Snow."

"The salt trains?" asked Ahanu.

"She married into the family."

The Snows were an old patriarchal-based family who had taken much of the property of the county by force from the Algonquin tribes in the 1600s. In the 1800s, the Snow Family built the Old Colony Railroad System. The railroad hauled salt and salt hay from the marshes to be processed and used for commercial enterprises in Boston and Manhattan. When the railroad closed, the Snows invested in glasswork factories, both sheet and bottle.

Ahanu agreed to the picture-taking.

Carrying the puppy, Ahanu walked with the doctor to his car parked at the pump. Shooting Star climbed up Ahanu's leather jacket. The doctor pulled his silver-and-gray camera from a leather case in the trunk and snapped a photo of the dog.

Whoosh! A panel flew out of the camera's front grill. The doctor palmed it into his hand.

"Now watch this," said the doctor with a grin. Ahanu came to his open palm.

The white doctor and the brown gas station owner regarded the milky square of paper in the doctor's hand.

A ripple ran across the paper. In the running, a shapeless dark form gathered, and from it, emerged a head. As the head sharpened into a nose and ears, a pair of black-and-white eyes arrived. While Ahanu stared in astonishment, the face of the puppy became clear. Ahanu drew his pointer finger over the dry edge of the photograph.

"Magic," he whispered.

"Polaroid," the doctor replied. "It's called a Polaroid Land Camera." He winked through the thick, round lenses of his eyeglasses. "It's the newest thing, and it's . . . science, Ahanu. Not romance."

"I am all for science, Dr. John, but science can never tell us why we find the stars so beautiful."

In the little square of the photograph, the personality of the rambunctious puppy emerged. "That's one cute canine, Ahanu. Let me see what the family thinks about the puppy. I'll ring you."

Of course, the family did not think very hard. Alice and Theo were overjoyed. Ted Snow did not care much . . . as long as Theo kept him quiet and out from under his feet.

The doctor rang Ahanu and told him the news.

For Theo, he would have to wait until the puppy was fully weaned before he could take him. But for now, Theo knew a face in the settled film from the doctor's instant camera. Dr. Cook gave him the Polaroid photo to keep. Theo pinned that Polaroid-face on his waking dream.

On Saturday, booted up in his waders, Theo walked down to the marshes. The mud surrounding the waters was a mangle of muck, intricately marked with the filigree of tracks and crab scrabbles. There were other footprints too—sandpipers, gulls, and oystercatchers. On the hill, the day was bright, so he wore his straw hat for shade. From his blue rucksack, Theo pulled out an old envelope from his great-aunt. Red-and-green stickers of elves and reindeers dotted it. From the envelope, he ritualistically, reverently, pulled the Polaroid of the puppy.

He propped the photograph in a cleft on the massive granite boulder he called 'Giant'. He had had many adventures with the boulder. Sometimes, Giant was a dragon. Other times he was a German tank. Occasionally, Giant was a planet from a strange galaxy.

Alice suggested to Theo that he exercise his imagination just like he exercised any of his muscles. Like his calves. Like his biceps. She helped Theo understand there were beautiful sinews to be found in a man other than the frightening sinews of his own father's battering arms.

"What good are we if we can't imagine?" she asked Theo.

She, like Ahanu, was a romantic. Perhaps that is why they were able to converse in a shared landscape of dream. Alice was a painter. "I'm not Sargent nor even Grant Wood," she told Theo with her knowing smile, "but I'm good enough. By selling portraits and landscapes, I can help put food on the table and oil in the furnace."

Theo stared at the black-and-white photograph of his puppy framed in the lichen-covered boulder. He cocked his straw brim back from his brow to get a better look. He observed the small gleam of light in each of the puppy's eyes, like the dabs of light in the eyes of all the portraits his mother painted.

He could not be certain of the color of the dog's fur as the photo was in black-and-white. In one daydream, he had seen his dog with dark gold fur. In the black-and-white polaroid, the hair looked lighter. There was no mistaking, however, the river of white that ran up the middle of the puppy's face. It congealed into an exploding star at the crown.

Theo stared at the photograph. He sensed the personality of the puppy. That dog was for him! He could almost feel the spirit of the puppy pushing against the four corners of the photograph.

The sun vanished behind a dense mist that overcame the marsh. Theo removed his straw hat. Laying it on the rough granite face of Giant, Theo began exercising his imagination. Giant was no longer a boulder. Giant grew into the Monomoy Gas Station. Out of the double doors of the station, the puppy flew. He was a willful rascal. He grabbed the rucksack at Theo's feet. He shook its shoulder-cord like prey, as if to shake the blue thing dead. *Yap! Yap!* He barked at Theo. He was off with the rucksack in his jaws, running into the cool, spring pools of the marsh. Theo charged after him.

"Give it back! Give it back!" Theo shouted. The puppy turned. He flashed his eyes in mischief. Theo caught the glance. With the rucksack firmly clamped in the small teeth of his tiny jaw, the puppy returned to his trajectory. The pup ran faster. Theo ran faster too. The animal reached a tide pool too deep for his legs. He paddled. Theo was surprised. *He could almost swim!*

Quickly, the rucksack took on the weight of the water. The black-and-white puppy slowed. Grabbing the puppy and the satchel into both arms, Theo laughed. With his waders, Theo slogged with the puppy through the water. Algae had colonized on the shores, giving the marsh an emerald cast. Sea lavender and samphire poked through the surface. Together, boy and dog came to solid ground.

Breathing hard, the puppy shivered in the boy's arms.

Rain fell into the grainy mist.

It was a deluge.

Theo had wanted to take his dog to visit the sea and meet his other friend, 'Red', a cedar tree of enormous size that grew on the bluff.

Together, they could sit beneath Red's canopy of growing leaves, watching the tremendous ocean froth like a leviathan in a fairy tale. They could listen to the gulls squawk as they soared. But, this was not the day. Theo picked up his wet rucksack from the marsh, slung it over his shoulder, and placed the puppy inside it.

For the first time, squeezing him close, Theo kissed the dog on his head. The puppy licked his rough tongue on his cheek and neck.

Theo looked at the puppy.

They had run. They had made mischief. They dreamed about seeing Red. Now, they were going to race home.

Theo grabbed his soaked straw hat, shoving it on his head. He pulled the Polaroid from the cleft in the rock. In streaks, the raindrops had almost obliterated the image of his dog.

Why do I need that photo, anyways? I have my puppy now.

Theo ran out of the marshes with the fervor only the very young can muster. He raced through the family graveyard and the trees that shaded it.

Next time, we'll go to the sea.

In the drenching rain, they ran up the hill toward the farm-house.

Theo had definitely exercised the muscle of his imagination. He was so full of joy over the coming of the dog he had not realized the dog had not yet fully arrived.

CHAPTER THREE

Before the little canines left for their forever homes, Ahanu Lightstone and Oota Dabun called for a blessing over the puppies. Having read *Peter Pan* to her grandchildren, Oota Dabun named the scraggly mother Wendy and her nurslings the Lost Boys. Husband and wife brought the pack of Lost Boys into an outdoor pen where the kid goats had been kept when first born. It was twilight. Ahanu lit a fire in a circle of stones next to the pen holding the excited puppies. What a difference five weeks made! The puppies had grown strong. They were now eight weeks old. Even Ahanu's runt, Shooting Star, had become robust. They hardly seemed lost. The little tigers ran inside the fencing—youngsters all, friendly competitors, with no leader yet, although each believed, of course, they were the leader.

The Lost Boys had never seen flames before. They were mesmerized by the fire glimmering inside the pit of the stone circle. The man who had been so warm to them was big against the red of the flames. When his huge hands beat his celebration drum, the rhythm rang not only in the pen but through the vast acreage of the Christmas tree farm. The happy drum song was a threshold ritual—opening a pathway bridge for the boys to a pleasant tomorrow.

Wearing a jangling necklace of small conch shells over a purple wool sweater, Oota Dabun bent down to the ground and lifted each puppy into her hands. She brushed warm cedar oil from a wooden bowl into the fur of the puppies. Her violet eyes sparkled as she looked earnestly at each of them.

Shooting Star sniffed at the bowl on the ground. He licked the bowl's wide mouth. It tasted delicious. But when the puppy dove into the bowl to consume more of the anointing oil, Oota Dabun laughed, sweeping him into her arms and rubbing his golden-brown fur with fragrant oil. Cedar was a balm used to strengthen and protect. It was believed to carry the good thoughts of the practitioners who administered it into the skin and blood of the recipients.

Theo's puppy listened to Oota Dabun as she wished him "good fortune" in her native tongue. But while the puppy did not know the Algonquin language, he knew the sacred meter of the Great Mother. Even though he could not see it, he understood the love that roils the cosmos. Oota Dabun snuggled him, covering him with the wonderful smell in her fingers. When she had finished rubbing all the brothers, she picked up the wooden bowl and left the pen.

With his large, dark eyes, Theo's puppy watched as the big man and the violet-eyed woman danced around the fiery circle of stone. They beseeched Gitche Manitou to release the guardian, Thunderbird. Gitche Manitou was a shapeless spirit. Thunderbird had form. He was a supernatural peregrine falcon. If the Lost Boys were ever in trouble, Thunderbird would beat his wings, booming like thunderous drums, and swoop down to save them.

Gada. Gada. Gada.

With the sizzling red-and-yellow light from the flames, the pounding of the drums—*gada, gada, gada*—and the voices of the masters of the farm lifted in music, Theo's puppy could not stop from dancing himself.

Yippee, he cried.

No longer overwhelmed by the flames, the puppy raced around the pen with his brothers. They barked as the Lightstones sang. Their beings hummed with the periodicity that sought able legs for the winding journey of their lives.

Yippee, the puppy cried again.

Gada. Gada. Gada.

In the days ahead, one by one, the brothers left one another.

Shooting Star was adamant. He would not vanish like the rest of his siblings. He was very clear to Mother Wendy about this.

In the stable, he fearfully hovered, remaining at her side, making certain no one could take him. Yes, there was Thunderbird to swoop down and save him. But who needed saving when Mom was at his side? He loved the way his mother licked him, how he could jump close into her fur, and how there was nothing in the whole moist earth as sweet as her milk, not even that cedar oil in Oota Dabun's wooden bowl. He was sad when all his mother's milk was gone. She was hard on him and his brothers. She sat on her teats, forcing her children to seek food from other sources.

Now, he was eating dry kibble and water from a bowl.

Blech!

"Things will change, son," Wendy told Shooting Star. "But while we may not always be together, we will always share each other's hearts."

"No need for that, Mom. I'm not leaving." Shooting Star talked to her in the ancient language of dog, not in words from the mouth but in images from the heart.

Whenever a new family came to pick up one of the Lost Boys, Shooting Star plunged his golden body into the unbundled yellow hay in the corner of the stable.

People thought he was being bashful.

"Aww," they sighed as they watched him dive into the straw.

But the puppy thought he was being strategic.

With all his brothers gone from the barn, he now hung on even more fervently to the idea that he was staying with his mother.

When we come to earth, we are all strangers and aliens. But Shooting Star felt even stranger with the loss of his six big brothers. He was born to play. And now, he was without playmates.

Now, he was truly the lost boy.

While his mother knew it was time for the puppy to go, that did not stop the little one from following her everywhere in the barn that sleepy Saturday morning.

When he heard the wheels of a car grind though the gravel driveway outside the barn, he fled from his mother, racing across the hard-packed dirt floor of the barn, pouncing into the straw of the stable. His yellow ears flopped against his round head. As the sliding door of the barn opened to white sunlight, the puppy watched from his hideout.

His mom walked to the mistress of the farm. Wendy greeted Oota Dabun by jumping on her and licking her with kisses.

What is Mom doing? Shooting Star thought. *She should be snarling! They are trying to take me away!*

Wendy was joined by a second woman. This was Alice Snow. And then there was someone bewildering who stood with her. He was half the size of the two women. The puppy tunneled into the hay as deep as he could and only his dark brown eyes shone out to scout the scene. Wendy sauntered over to the corner of the hay pile and told him to come to her.

Shooting Star could not disobey the bark of his mother.

"Aww, poor little fella. He's scared," said the half-sized human. The puppy felt a tad better. At least the creature was not calling him "bashful." Whatever that meant.

As his mom continued to bark, Shooting Star pulled his head out farther. He was a portrait coming out of a gilded frame of straw. Wide, frightened eyes. A golden head with an arrow of white that rose to a star-splotch upon his crown.

With her cold nose and her warm head, his mom nuzzled him, coaxing him out of the hay. She told him it was time to start his great journey.

"Must I go, Mom?" the puppy asked.

"It is what you were born to do—to be with the humans," Wendy said in animal-cant.

"But how do I do that, Mom? I do not know how. I should stay with you until I learn," the puppy argued.

"Do not fear, son."

She said it so softly, so empathetically, that, somehow, it was enough. Shooting Star clambered out of the straw and down the slope of the pile to his mommy who stood at the edge of it.

She nuzzled his snout one last time with her cold black nose.

"Go, son," she said.

He stood there, frozen in confusion.

"Go."

He could hear her love in her barking throat. Her sweet tone gave him the impetus to move.

Do not fear.

Reluctantly, he scampered across the dirt-packed floor of the barn to the feet of Oota Dabun. He liked the mistress of the gasoline farm. With her two hot hands, she picked up the puppy. She brushed his healthy nose against her warm one.

So hot and different from my mom's whiffer, thought the puppy.

"I will miss you, my kizis," Oota Dabun said as she held him close to her.

She leaned down and handed Shooting Star to the half-sized human. The puppy observed finally that the half-sized human was a youngster, too, probably not much older than he. His hair was short to match his height. He had brown hair and green eyes. He wore some muddy-colored contraption around his eyes that was tethered to his ears. The puppy would later learn they were called "eyeglasses."

"Oh, you have saved the best for last," said Alice cheerily looking down at the dog. "What adorable markings he has! Look, you could call him Arrow by those markings!"

"Ahanu calls him Shooting Star," said Oota Dabun. "But you, Theo, will find the name that is right for the two of you."

Shooting Star had never seen a boy up close before, so

he was curious about such a creature. Even in his fear, the puppy stared at the boy. The boy smelled of soap and mud and sugar. The puppy did not realize it then, but he was staring at his life, his destiny. *Master Theodore Joseph Snow from the shores of New England. Reader. Farmer. Pupil. Son. Comic-book lover. Ice cream maniac. Boy. Home.* The puppy watched as Oota Dabun gave the strange lady a towel. He was a bit confused for the lady was also called Mom by the boy. Towels were soft things that the puppy liked to clamp his teething, aching mouth into and wrassel with his brothers. But this was not for wrasseling.

"He has never ridden in a car, so he is bound to throw up and, perhaps, not just once. Do you have a windup alarm clock? If not, pick one up at Kresge's. Wind it up and wrap it in a T-shirt at night. This will keep him from crying. The ticking will remind him of his mother's heartbeat. The rhythm will help him sleep."

"That sounds fun," barked the puppy, whining in the confused growing consciousness of self.

As Theo walked into the yard next to the barn, a great shadow fell across his path. It was Ahanu Lightstone. To Theo, his face seemed as hard as the boulder named Giant.

"I have but four words for you," the tall man said. He was dressed in his leather motorcycle jacket, his long hair tied in a ponytail at his neck.

"Four words?" asked Theo, thrown off guard.

"Dogs were once wolves."

Furrowing his brow, Theo pondered what the imposing man

had just said. "What do you mean?"

"Wolves stood outside our fires, and humans were terrified," answered Ahanu. "Yet our warrior-fathers did not kill them. The wolves came from Mother Earth. They were part of us. So, we brought what we feared to the warmth of the flame. Before the fire, we trained them. We loved them. We bred them to be useful to our tribes. Over the many years, what had frightened us now became our greatest allies. Together, these dogs and we people fought against the darkness of the wood."

Theo blinked, trying to understand. He looked at the golden puppy on the ground, running through the feet and legs of the adults. Then to Ahanu. "But, sir, why do you tell me this?" Theo asked.

"This dog, who shall be under your care, belongs to the best of humankind's creation. For man transformed that which he feared into something which could love him. The dog, Theo, is the great witness to the one truth. There is but the one truth. Four words like my tale. The truth is this: Love triumphs over fear. Remember what I say for I know you. Do not ask me how I know that you live in a storm of fury . . ." Then he said softly, intimately, ". . . and fear. But take heart, for love has overcome the wild world. Dogs were once wolves."

While Ahanu spoke, the puppy made his way to Theo's side. He wound in and out of his legs, batting, experimentally, at the boy's shoelaces. Then the puppy flopped on his side at the boots of Ahanu.

"Treat the dog well, and he will be your guide," said Ahanu.

Theo smiled and reached down and petted the puppy. Theo had heard that Mister Lightstone was a medicine man. His family had lived in the shore regions for thousands of years. Theo looked at him. He felt the strength of the man, but he also felt his kindness.

"Your dog is our favorite, but he was meant for you, not for us," said Ahanu as he crouched down to pet the puppy. He rubbed the puppy's white crown. "My wife and I saw your mother calling for this dog in a dream. We have had many adventures, Theo Snow. Now, it is time for you to have your adventure. This sacred dog will guide you on the road. For there is no road but for the one you and he shall make by walking. It is your road. It is no one else's road. Take heart in your steps for such steps lead you to your life. And this sacred one shall help you find your North Star."

"Really?" said Theo. "This puppy is sacred?"

"You know that!" Ahanu said, his voice rising in power. Theo put his arm over his face, fearful that the man might whack him. "Do not hide. All life is sacred! Even the blessed earth you take into your mouth."

Theo felt ashamed. He put his hand down. No one was going to hit him. Alice looked astonished as Theo glanced at her. But he knew her respect for the man kept her from speaking. Theo breathed deeply, rebounding from Ahanu's brashness. Ahanu was a medicine man, after all. It was probably his duty to talk about sacredness and fear and fires burning through the ages.

As he stood in front of the wise man, Theo thought about all the dogs that he had ever looked at, truly looked at. Theo recalled in their eyes a dark road that held no horizon, only endlessness.

Was that eternity?

"Yes, sir, I do know that all life is sacred," Theo said. "We learn that at church, sometimes in books, and in my Boy Scout troop." Theo's voice grew sincere. "Thank you for allowing me to have him." He felt his mother's hand on his shoulder. "I will take good care of him," Theo said. "I promise you."

Ahanu looked at Alice as if for her acceptance. She nodded. To Theo, it was as if they had had a conversation about what was yet to be.

"Then swear your oath to me," said the medicine man.

Theo knew, from all the books he read, there was an epoch of humankind before written history. Without papyrus or paper, men and women pledged their spoken word to one another. And if they foreswore the oath, their tongue would be cut from their mouths. Theo swallowed. The taste of blood was on his lips. He did not want to have his tongue cut out by the man.

"Swear to me!" Ahanu commanded.

"I swear my oath that I shall take good care of him."

"Good," Ahanu replied. He picked up the puppy playing on the ground. He handed Shooting Star to Theo. The puppy easily went to the boy. Theo cradled him in his arms. The puppy looked at Theo, snapped, and then started licking him. Theo laughed, swiping the wet kiss from his cheek. Ahanu reached into Theo's arms, scruffing the dog under his chin.

"With care, the dog will embrace you," Ahanu said. "In his bones, the dog knows the journey to shed the fur of the wolf. You must do the same. The anger inside you must give way."

"Anger?"

Ahanu looked carefully at the boy. He spoke softly, carefully. "Master the dog, Theo. In mastering the dog, you shall learn to master yourself."

The puppy perched in Theo's arms like a parcel of grain, limp, leaning in, sniffing at the soapy smell behind the boy's ears.

Alice and Theo said their thanks and their goodbyes and

walked to the station wagon.

Theo placed the golden ball of striped fluff into a small cardboard box in the back seat of his mom's car. There was a small lambskin in the box on which the puppy could rest. But as the car rumbled, the pup was overwhelmed with melancholy and the newness of the bouncing tires against the rocky road. He was leaving his mom behind. His dark eyes blinked— wide and wild. *All alone.* When he smelled the lambskin upon which he sat, he cried for the soul of the slaughtered sheep.

"Do you have any idea what you will name him, Theo?" Alice asked as they drove away from the Monomoy station and farm. Theo looked up from the back seat. He noticed the seashell clip in his mom's auburn hair. He had given it to her for her twenty-ninth birthday.

"Not yet, Mom. I guess we'll have a name once we get to know him."

The small corrugated walls of the cardboard box knocked against Shooting Star's body.

Theo looked down at the miserable youngster sitting in the box on his lap. "There, there, puppy. It's going to be okay." The quiet voice of the boy could not keep the dog from hurling his kibble into the box.

"Blech," Theo cried, blanching.

"Sweetie, what's wrong?" asked Alice as she drove through the dirt roads back to Blueberry Hill.

"Puppy threw up."

The puppy looked up and hurled another stream of mashed

kibble directly into Theo's face.

The stream was so noxious that Theo was seized with an instant reflex. He picked the puppy up and vomited into the cardboard box.

"I think we need some fresh air." Theo wiped his mouth with the towel. He rolled down the backseat window.

"Stay steady, Theo. We'll be home in a minute," Alice said soothingly.

When they reached the Snow farmhouse, Alice ran to the back seat and opened the door. She took Theo and his puppy away from the box and onto the front lawn. It was early June, so it was warm. She turned the green garden hose on both the boy and the puppy until they were clean. Then, as Theo shook along with the puppy, she held out the messy lambskin and hosed it down too.

In the kitchen, Alice revved up her Handy Hannah Hair Dryer she had bought with her ration stamps two years ago. She sat Theo in a chair while he held the puppy. As the hot motor whirled, the hair dryer blew the puppy and boy dry. Theo watched his mom work. She had dressed nicely for her meeting at the Lightstone's. She wore a white dress printed with small lavender petunias.

Later, Theo sat in the grass on Blueberry Hill and played with the puppy. There was no fencing or leash necessary since the dog was only eight weeks old. He could not run far. Theo ran his thumb over the furry star at the top of the dog's head. He petted his two front legs. The puppy wrasseled with a fetch rope while Theo pulled on one end and the puppy pulled on the other.

While the boy was different from his six brothers and had absolutely no fur on him, the puppy sensed that the boy, too, was a stranger. He observed Theo looking at the house in fear as if he did not belong there. Some deep instinct drew the dog to the boy. He burrowed into the small nook between his chest and his arm. He breathed him in. He adored him with a thousand sandpaper kisses. Then, bored, Shooting Star went back to the fetch rope.

In a while, he was exhausted from the roughhousing. Theo may have been half-sized but he was a lot stronger than puppy's brothers. Shooting Star dropped the rope and plopped into the lawn.

A caterpillar in the deep sleeves of the grass caught the attention of the pup. Theo gently parted the sleeves so the pup could see him better. Theo watched as he pounced over the furry, wriggling larva, mantling like a peregrine over prey. Theo pulled on his neck fur so the dog would not eat the creature. Immediately, the puppy calmed down. He watched with curiosity. Boy and pup sat, caught for an instant in some magic moment of communion. They both understood the dreamy consciousness of the larva—her butterfly wings breaking the walls of the cocoon, her kaleidoscopic wings flying upward.

Puppy lay on his back in the grass like an upturned table. His white paws hung in midair. He fell asleep in a sunbeam.

Theo gently picked up the sleeping animal. He folded the puppy into a crate from Sears & Roebuck on the floor in the kitchen. He closed the steel grating, so the puppy could sleep quietly and become accustomed to the crate.

While the puppy slept, as pups do for hours to accommodate the growth spurts, Theo walked into town. He passed the lighthouse, the Mayflower Hotel, and the public library. At Kresge's Five and Dime, he bought a windup alarm clock. He turned its key to be certain it worked. It *ticked, ticked, ticked*. He then paid the cashier the twenty-three cents.

"What are you going to name the puppy?" asked Veronica Simms, the young cashier at the five and dime. She looked just like the blonde film star Veronica Lake, for whom she was named. Just like the star of the silver screen, her hair fell over one eye like a gold-plated waterfall.

"I thought I would wait until he told me," Theo answered, pushing his horn-rim glasses up the bridge of his nose.

"I see," pretty Veronica said. "That's what happened with my little Lilac. She loved fetching Lilac stalks."

"Better that she liked lilacs rather than beef jerky," Theo replied with a smile.

Veronica looked at the boy, confused.

"Here, Beef Jerky. Here, girl," Theo said to answer the question in Veronica's eyes. He was only eleven, but he liked Veronica. Finally, Veronica laughed. Theo took his purchase in the paper bag and left the five and dime, feeling like he was a man, king of his world.

Chapter Four

That night, heartsick for his mom, Shooting Star whined in his crate. He missed her warm fur and belly, fragrant with heat. In remembering, the puppy recalled how patient his mom had been when he couldn't stand on all fours. She was there for him, nudging him upward with her nose against his rump until he could not only stand but also take his first steps. It didn't matter that he was the last Lost Boy to stand. It didn't matter that he was the runt of the litter. His beautiful mother loved him just the same. As he lay in his crate, the puppy wept for her, for the life that had been, for the life he had known, for a mother's love that overlooked his impossible shortcomings.

How can I live without Mom? he wondered. He was but a bundle of longing. He didn't even understand it.

Whatever this new adventure was, the puppy did not like it. He yearned to return to his mom's warmth.

"Have no fear," his phantom mother said softly to him as he squirmed in his crate.

But as he held up his paw to touch her face, the paw

swiped right through the fevered phantasm. His cry raged all the wilder as the specter proved no more than illusion.

When the puppy heard foot falls in the dark kitchen, he looked out from the front of the crate through the crosshatch of steel. In the moonlight slanting through the kitchen window, he saw the boy with bare feet walk toward him.

The boy held the lambskin in his hand, all clean and dry. In the other hand, he held a cloth with a thump-thump-thump-thump within. When the boy placed the thumping into his crate with the good-smelling animal skin, the puppy nestled his little side right up to it. *Thump-thump-thump-thump.*

Instantly, the puppy liked where he was. He was grateful for what the boy had done. He laid his head against the magical rhythm of his mother's heart.

Thump-thump-thump-thump.

Tick-tock–tick-tock.

Thump-thump-thump-thump.

This was not a specter. This was his mother's heart manifest by his side. Every rhythm prepares a future. To the reassuring measure, the puppy fell asleep.

At first light, Theo returned.

He took the puppy right out of his crate, ran outside, and placed him as fast as he could on the cold, dew-drenched grass so he could pee. This was a good thing. The puppy could hardly hold it any longer. As the grass steamed, he barked with relief.

Theo patted the puppy's head and scruffed his neck. "What a good boy you are. Yes, you sure are." Puppy was thrilled with the praise. He was so excited that he lay down in the grass near where he wet and rolled over hoping that he would get a tummy rub from the boy.

Sure enough, he got the tummy rub.

The boy seemed to be having fun too. As the boy stroked the puppy's tummy, the puppy licked the salt and soap from the boy's ear. Theo laughed.

O' what a laugh! The puppy liked the boy. He thought he might teach him to play just like his other brothers. He was a natural-born leader, after all. The boy picked him up and held him close and whispered into his ear, "I love you, puppy. You are a good boy." *There is something about that voice*, thought the dog. Suddenly, he was excited about his new home.

My mom was right, the puppy thought. *This will be a good adventure!*

As soon as the tall woman or the boy would pull him out of his cozy den with his lambskin and thumping heart, he was taken into the great world of grass and tree and cerulean-blue skies.

Yippee, he cried.

It was grand on the mount that the humans called Blueberry Hill. In the eminence of Nature, the puppy sensed the great falcon, Thunderbird, unfurling his tremendous wings, soaring in the merry morning, watching over him. The puppy lay in the sunny grass and observed the beetles. The white-breasted robin warbled from her branch on the sweetgum tree.

The boy took the puppy to his mother's vegetable and flower garden. The bees droned in the breathing flora, their wings drenched in the consciousness of their species. The pup loved the reliable cadence of their buzz. The garden became a favorite spot for the youngster. He loved smelling the lettuces and peonies as they unfolded in the sun.

He loved the compost pile too. Theo, not so much. The damp underbelly of the leaves intoxicated the puppy as he burrowed deep in the leafy and weedy mound. When the puppy was sated, he came and sat on his haunches next to Theo who, following a swim, lay in the grass next to the pond.

"You're like my shadow," Theo said, idly scratching behind the puppy's ears.

Shooting Star was given a collar. He walked with a leash from time to time, especially near the road, which he did not like. He strained on the leash, for he had gotten much bigger. Theo did not want him running away.

At the marsh near the great rock, Giant, Theo often played with Shooting Star. The puppy loved chasing the grackles, juncos, and egrets in the warm pools. "Mom's right, boy . . . about exercising your imagination like a muscle. 'Cause look—here we are!" said Theo in a trumpeting voice. They were together in the real world, experiencing the beauty that had once only been a dream.

"Come on! I want you to see this," Theo said. Today, Giant was the great lighthouse to the world. Often, Theo saw for miles from the lighthouse porch. Many times, he viewed the most incredible sights—bears, seals on the rocks, whales in the sea.

He had no idea what they might see today, but whatever it was, it was certain to be wonderful. He pulled the puppy into his arms, cradling him like a papoose. Carefully, he scaled the rock face carrying the dog. When they stood on the summit of Giant, Theo set the dog down.

Together, they looked. A mother deer and her two yearlings had broken from the snarl of the bramble near the shoreline to the sea. They moved across a bluff and passed into a soft curtain of milkweed and dandelion seeds. They were white tails. Their tails bounced as they reached the ocean. "I've never seen deer on sand before," said Theo in studious awe. As for the dog, his tail shot up. It waved like a Fourth of July flag to greet them.

Later, as Theo and he walked the same beach, there were the hoofprints of the deer and her fawns. Shooting Star lowered his nose meticulously into the shallow dampness of the mother deer's track. He shut his eyes as if listening. Theo realized it was smell he was listening to. The wild, high-flying music of smell that he knew so little about.

As Shooting Star grew, he noticed that the thumping heart was not as steadfast as his mother's. Every day, when the boy pulled the heart from the dog's home, the puppy heard something turning, cranking at the side of the crate. Then, the boy would put the heart back into his cave-home. For the first part of the day, the thumping was constant. Then it would slow down until the boy returned, conjuring some kind of magic with that cranking noise. The heart came back into the crate, fixed and thumping just like mom's.

It wasn't until Shooting Star started really teething that he learned the truth. His poor teeth seemed to be pushing through his jaw like sunflowers in the field.

Pushing, pushing upward!

That hurts!

To quell the pain, the puppy pounced on picket fences, shoes, socks, ropes, or anything that he could sink his teeth into.

O' that feels good!

But one night, the pain of teething collided with the puppy's growing suspicion of his mother's thumping heart.

The humans had gone to bed. As his teeth were bothering him so, puppy couldn't sleep. He lunged into the lambskin and roughhoused with it. He pulled on the cloth that surrounded his mother's heart. He pulled and pulled so hard that the knotted cloth came undone, revealing the red and horrible face of a machine.

The machine-mommy donned a silver dome ringer at the top of her round body. Her face, etched in ancient writings and numbers, was so terrible that she held her silver hands over her face to hide her wretchedness. *That is not my mommy's heart!* He whimpered in the crate. *Since it is not mommy, I am going to chew those horrible hands to stop my pain!*

When Theo heard the puppy's yelping, he grabbed his eyeglasses and tumbled down the stairs. Padding through the front hallway, he entered the kitchen with its wide-planked floors. He could not see the puppy through the crosshatch grill, but he could certainly hear him yelping.

Crouching down on the floor, Theo stared through the grill. He observed Shooting Star's body cowering at the back of the crate. He was huffing air as if choking. The alarm clock had been torn apart, lying at the front of the crate. In the muted moonlight, Theo saw Shooting Star with his mouth wide open in a perpetual gasp. It took Theo only a moment to discover that there was something gleaming in the puppy's mouth. The long hand of the clock was lodged between his lower jaw and the roof of his mouth. It was prying his mouth wide open.

Theo unfastened the crate. At first, he planned to pull the puppy out, but the dog looked at him with such panic, Theo thought the better of it. The move might cause him to swallow the long hand of the clock. Theo had no idea what that would mean, but he thought it just might kill the defenseless little fella.

"There, there," Theo said with as much tenderness as he could muster, not knowing how else to calm his puppy. "There, there."

Quietly but quickly, Theo walked across the kitchen to the junk drawer by the sink. He plucked a set of small pliers from it. He returned to the crate and reached inside.

With his left hand, Theo gently opened up Shooting Star's jaw so that his hand and fingers became stronger tension surrounding the little dog's mouth. With his right hand on the pliers, Theo pinched the silver hand and yanked it from the puppy's jaw, blood splattering against his fingers. The puppy screeched. Then, almost instantaneously, he stopped whining. Theo warmed some water on the stove and allowed the dog to drink the soothing liquid from a ladle as he gently stroked his head.

"There, there."

Having wrapped him in his lambskin blanket, Theo climbed the moon-painted stairs. He brought the puppy onto his bed. Theo took off his glasses and lay down on the mattress. The puppy sniffed about the sheets and peered over the side of the bed, observing the height of this new locale. The puppy turned, dancing across the mattress, nestling up against Theo's ribcage.

Theo marveled at how fast the little one had moved from trauma to joy. Theo breathed deeply, relieved that the operation had been successful. But there was something more that was travelling through the precocious boy. He had become empathetic. Together, Theo and Shooting Star had shared a great pain. Together, they had come through the other side of it. He sighed with relief as the puppy lay against his body. His eyes swelled with fiery tears and with pride, accomplishment, and humility. In the small struggles of life, great deeds are often committed. For Theo, this was one of those small and great feats.

By his side, the puppy grew silent, listening to the steady *thump-thump-thump-thump* of the boy's heart. Theo held him close and breathed the dog into him.

Theo stroked the dog's head, whispering. *There, there. There, there.* Theo looked at his hand. The puppy was asleep under his palm, stretched against his thigh, lightly snoring. Theo felt the warmth against his leg. *There, there.* As he listened to his shallow snoring, Theo loved him.

CHAPTER FIVE

"What was doin' with your dog last night?" asked Ted. He walked through the kitchen and passed Theo at the breakfast table. Alice stood at the sink, finishing up last night's dishes.

"I'm sorry. He was sick." Theo replied as he ate his Cheerios, staring at the back of the cereal box.

"You have to get that dog under control. I need my shut-eye, champ. Those were the rules, remember? No pissing in my house. No yapping. Okey dokey?"

"Okey dokey," replied Theo.

"Otherwise, that dog is going to be in the house at the back of the barn like every other Snow dog."

Theo did not answer, nor did he look at his father.

"Can you remember you agreed to pay for his food and his rabies shots as well?" Ted said or asked. Theo was not quite sure. With his father, he learned simply to answer the requisite questions without emotion.

"I remembered. That's why I took on extra yard work with the McCormicks," he said, staring at the back of the cereal box. "I even learned how to use Mr. McCormick's snow plow for the winter."

"Theo is helping every week," said Alice.

Ted turned to Alice as he grabbed his jacket from the hook near the kitchen door. "I don't want one cent coming from the house account to take care of that pooch. Understood?"

"I understand," she said. Theo bristled at the way his father demeaned his mother.

"Don't worry, Dad," said Theo.

"If it wakes me up one more time in the middle of the night, that little beast is sleeping in the little house where it belongs, do you hear me?" he said. He frowned importantly.

"He's not an it. It's a he."

"Do you hear me, champ?" Ted repeated.

"I hear you, Dad," Theo replied. He watched his father's fidget finger. As was the habit, the finger nervously contract-ed and opened as if the appendage had a life of its own. His father walked through the kitchen door without another word. He was wearing his bomber jacket and pilot shades. *All dressed up for flying, but his plane is grounded!* Theo smirked. The door squeaked its condemning squeak.

"How is the dog this morning?" Alice asked.

Theo looked down to see Shooting Star at his feet chomp-ing on buttered toast. He loved buttered toast. He seemed oblivious to the pain he experienced the night before. Theo reached down and petted the dog. With his dark liquid eyes, the puppy looked at him.

"He's fine."

Shooting Star looked at Alice. Gone was the moon-head rendered by the yellow, floppy ears flat against his skull. His ears now stood upright. Alice looked at her son in surprise.

"It happened overnight," replied Theo. "I guess it's like when human legs grow. I wonder if it hurt like my legs sometimes do."

Theo ate some more cereal from his spoon. "I guess puppy's not a puppy anymore."

Alice attempted to break the anxiety churning in the wake of Ted's departure. "Are you ever going to name him?" she asked with a smile in her voice. She had that magic of changing the atmosphere.

"I don't want to make the same mistake you and dad made with my name," Theo replied. "I don't want to give him a name that I will later regret."

"But you are Theo, not Ted," replied Alice, soothingly. "Must you hold on to that?"

"Ted, Theodore, Theo, Teddy—don't you get it? They, we, are all the same," he said in frustration, turning his green eyes back to the Cheerios box. "I will always be attached to *him*."

"What's in a name anyways?" she said with a laugh.

"Plenty. Just ask Romeo Montague and Juliet Capulet what's in a name. Their names killed them."

"Your name is not going to kill you," Alice replied.

"Probably not," Theo said grimly.

At school that day, Theo worried that his father might do more than just put the dog in the old dog house. He was concerned that Ted would hurt the puppy. When he fell asleep in math class, having been up most of the night with the dog, Theo had that very nightmare.

Wailing its dark tidings, the storm arrived.

The storm killed the dog.

Rather than taking the school bus, Theo walked home that afternoon. He found that walking gave him ideas. But the ideas were slow to come. Ahead of him were the encroaching, high spirals of the Snow Glassworks factory. The smokestacks spewed their ghostly, atomic totems of toxic cadmium and arsenic. His own dark thoughts could easily have been swept into the poisonous smoke of the reality all around him. Instead, he sought the restful beauty of the countryside. The violet light of the afternoon sun shone on the dirt road. The sniff of the wheat in the fields tethered Theo to Nature.

By the time he reached the blue door of the farmhouse, he was determined that the puppy not cause his father to lose any sleep or bring him to anger. First, he hung his rucksack in the mud room.

Then, Theo freed the puppy from his crate in the kitchen and hurried him to his afternoon constitution in the yard. "We are a team, get it?" said Theo. Just to be sure the puppy understood what the two of them were facing, Theo walked him behind the barn.

There was the iron post with a ring and chain. Next to it was an old dog shelter with a derelict, peaked roof and walls suffering from dry rot. "We don't want this to become your home, pup," Theo said. The two of them stared at the house of disrepair. "No, boy, you aren't gonna live like that. We need to figure this out together."

What an awful place. The puppy shivered. He barked.

"I agree, pup. No place like home. Yikes." Theo gave a tug

on his leash. "No boy, you aren't living like that."

In his bedroom, Theo opened the cupboard next to the hearth. It was used to store firewood in the old days, but now it was empty. This would be a safe place. He could keep an eye on Shooting Star and make sure there was no "pissing." No "yapping." Little did Theo know he was also creating a safe place for himself.

"For me and my shadow," said Theo. The dog looked at Theo. "Does that work for you, boy?" The puppy jumped, fixing his paws on Theo's lap. He reached up and licked his face, letting out whimpers of joy. "Then Shadow it is."

While the puppy watched from a corner of the room, Theo propped an iron Superman door stop, painted blue and red, against the wooden door of the hearth closet to keep it open. He swept the small floor of the cupboard free of wood chips and spider webs, making it neat and tidy. Then he lay the lambskin from the crate in the four corners of the cupboard. It fit almost perfectly. Theo stood back from his work, pleased.

"Whaddaya think, Shadow? Do you think this will work as your new cubby?" asked Theo. "Superman will keep it open for you, and you can come and go as you please. You'll sleep up here in my room with me, so I can make sure you stay quiet at night."

Shadow sniffed the strange locale, his black nose trembling from his fast-cinching nostrils. Then, he sat outside the cupboard as if in protest. From his pocket, Theo pulled a fistful of Cheerios. He held his fist closed as he brought it to Shadow's sensitive nose.

He lured Shadow into his new home with the smell of the oat cereal. Theo sprinkled the Cheerios at the back of the lamb blanket. Nostrils flaring, Shadow walked to the far end of the cubby. He munched up his oat feast, dabbing his wet mouth against the lambskin.

Shadow turned in his cubby. He lay down, staring out from his new home at Theo's room. After consideration, Shadow thought he had arrived at a most remarkable new land.

The toys!

He gazed out from his soft, safe domain to glimpse tin planes, a small white wooden boat with a rudder, Lincoln Logs, a silver Ferris Wheel constructed from magic known as an Erector Set, a rocket made of steel, and lots of rubber balls to play with, including what were known as a baseball, football, tennis ball, and soccer ball. There were also shelves and shelves of what he would later learn were called books. They were bound in all kinds of sizes and had ancient symbols on their spines.

The Puppy Book gave Theo instructions on how to get Shadow to stick close to him. Theo knew his puppy really disliked the strain of the leash. The answer was found in a glass jar of Peter Pan Peanut Butter. Since he was a Lost Boy and knew Peter Pan from the tales of his Algonquin mistress, this lesson plan made perfect sense to Shadow.

The boy slathered the magic butter on an old, wooden mixing spoon and held it to his side. The spoon's handle was long enough to stretch below Theo's knee. Theo repeated "walk with me" again and again. Shadow did not even have to jump to get to the savory ecstasy. *Theo is so kind*, thought Shadow.

"Walk with me. Walk with me," Theo said. Sometimes he said, "Walk with me, buddy" or, at other times, "Walk with me, pal."

Why wouldn't I walk with you? wondered Shadow. *You have that delicious, mouth-watering butter!*

They sauntered up and down Blueberry Hill, Shadow following

the alchemy of the mouth-watering butter everywhere.

Then there was a time when the spoon wasn't there, but still Theo would say "Walk with me." And Shadow would walk with Theo even without the Peter Pan Peanut Butter.

Shadow eventually forgot about the savory butter.

All he needed was the boy.

And for Shadow, that pesky leash was gone.

Together, they quested on blissful idylls through the samphire of the salt marshes and the sparkling sand of the seashore. Theo's great childhood rock, Giant, became forty different rocks—a fort, a mountain, a spaceship, a glittering castle, Jupiter, Mars.

All Theo needed to do was say, "walk with me." Shadow would bolt up from wherever he was. He would start running in place with excitement, the white paws battering up and down in fevered bliss. Sometimes, Shadow walked so close, Theo felt his saunter, almost like an embrace. They were linked like a nucleus and an electron.

Theo often walked barefoot. He loved the cold ooze of the marsh at his toes. He felt the knowingness of the wild grass against his foot pads. Beneath his growing body, toiling the deep soil, the earthworms wriggled, ruled by the thrumming of consciousness reserved especially for their species. The rhythms shot straight to his own body. When he walked barefoot with Shadow, he felt the connection between him, his dog, and the heaven beneath his feet. He felt the connection not only with his dog but with all dogs. Theo recalled what Ahanu had told him. "For there is no road but for the one you and he shall make by walking. That is your road." Theo often thought that when he walked through the landscape with his dog. He walked into his own self. He felt the crisp wind outside himself and inside himself. It was a happy refreshment.

Often, when Shadow chased the tide of the beach, his tail wagging high like a banner, Theo sat on the bluff beneath the blue-green branches of the cedar tree that Shadow and he called Red. Under the spreading canopy of leaves and scampering squirrels, Theo watched the dog. Shadow delighted in chasing the ebb and flow of the ocean.

"Do you want me to tell you a bedtime story?" Theo asked Shadow. The dog lay majestically in his throne room in the hearth cupboard. There was a shelf that had many books, in red, plum, and green, beyond just the single puppy book.

Yippee, replied Shadow, although he was not entirely sure what a story was. He thought it might be part of the *big adventure* his mom had talked to him about. Theo kneeled before the shelf and looked at what he proudly called his "library."

"How about I read *Lassie Come Home?*" asked Theo.

Shadow barked enthusiastically, not sure who Lassie was.

"Lassie is a dog like you," answered Theo.

Yippee.

For a while, the dog simply cocked his head this way and then that way, uncertain of what Theo was saying.

But soon, Shadow fell into the ancient cadences between man and wolf, those rhythms that rippled beyond words, that mysterious spirit-cant between the domains of humans and animals.

When he crossed into the deep river of that meter, Shadow understood almost everything that Theo had to say. Shadow's eyes went wide as he sat in his little cubby listening to *Lassie Come Home*. Theo was very entertaining in telling tales, using different voices for the many characters. The telling affected Shadow.

Theo had a good, low growl for the mythic collie, Lassie. He spun a funny lilt in his voice when he spoke like Mrs. Carraclough, the mom. Shadow shuddered when Mrs. Carraclough said, "You might as well know it right off, Joe. Lassie won't be meeting you at school anymore."

"Why not?" asked Joe. Joe was the boy. "What's happened?"

Theo even shook when he spoke in a rattling voice, "Lassie's been sold, son."

The poor Carracloughs had no money, so they had to barter the dog to make ends meet. Shadow listened anxiously over the days and weeks to follow. When Lassie was sold, all Lassie wanted to do was get back to her boy, Joe.

As Shadow and Theo fell into the story, they shared something in common, beyond pain, between them: an exciting adventure where they never had to leave the room.

Lassie wanted to get back to Joe. Lassie's dark journey took her through fire, peril, and even terrible storms.

"I know something about this dog," a woman said as she looked at Lassie. "She's going somewhere, and she's on her way."

Shadow was relieved when Lassie jumped the equestrian fence and entered the yard to the Carraclough home, returning to Joe.

Yippee, he barked.

Theo closed the book on the final page. Theo was not sure if Shadow was barking because the story was over or because he now wanted a new story.

"What is the answer?" Theo asked Shadow.

Shadow barked twice.

"Probably both, right?" Theo asked. "Miss Pryor, in English, says that one book might end but the story goes on in other books. 'For life and literature are one,' Miss Pryor says. 'The story moves through us all and is never ending. All creatures great and small are bound together in the one never-ending story.'"

Yippee, Shadow barked.

When Theo finished a book that was not on the shelf, Shadow and he would walk to the center of town. Theo admired the strong step of the dog. Shadow was everything Theo wanted to be—singular, self-possessed, free from grief, and numb to the hurts of human life.

Along the way, Shadow always liked to wade in Oyster Pond. He lifted his leg on the stone foundation to the lighthouse. In town, there stood a massive temple known as the "library." It was much larger than Theo's shelves. The public library was painted white with a wide porch for sitting. Like the "good boy" he was, Shadow would wait by the double green doors for the boy while he returned one book and picked up another.

"What do you feel like, Shadow? A story with adventure, suspense, rite of passage?" Theo asked him.

Shadow did not care. He did not bark approval. He simply yawned in comfort. He loved them all. Humans are such complicated creatures, thought Shadow. Their stories matched their entangled lives with all sorts of challenges and paradoxes.

Dogs longed for consistency and simplicity. They wanted to love and be loved. Every once in a while, they would also like to have a good bone to gnaw on.

They read *Huckleberry Finn, Look Homeward, Angel, The Jungle Book,* and even George Orwell's *Animal Farm.* Theo acted out all the parts on the farm—the tyrannical Berkshire boar, Napoleon, and his chief propagandist, Squealer, a plump, white porker. Although Shadow admired the story, he did not feel the author of the story quite understood animal-cant.

Unlike the neighborhood houses around Cockle Cove, the town square had a diversity of buildings—some brick, some in wood with ecclesiastical steeples. This was New England. Every town had three or four churches. Shadow would sit in the grass on Sunday morning while the Snows went to a church. They entered a building with an old ship mast built into its steeple. There were also drugstores and haberdasheries and bars and the A&P grocery store. And of course, the temple called "library."

After the trip to the library, if he was an especially good boy and the weather was warm, Shadow got an icy, savory treat. He waited outside Saywells Drugstore while Theo went inside and purchased an ice cream in a cone. They would walk across the street into the park. There, they would sit together on an old weather-beaten wooden bench.

Theo would take a lick and then Shadow would have his. "It's called sharing," Theo explained to the dog. "You get one and then I get one. Don't try to butt-in when I am having my lick, though, get it, buddy?" When they finished their ice cream, the dog inevitably eating the final bit of waffle, Theo and his dog would sing and bark the jingle of post-war America:

I scream. You scream. We all scream for ice cream!

I scream. You scream. We all scream for ice cream!

Sometimes, when Theo did not feel like reading at night, he and Shadow would listen to Theo's favorite stories on the

Star Raider radio made by the Continental Radio Corporation.

The Star Raider, a scalloped oval with a star at the top of its curve, grandly perched on Theo's bureau. It had pretty good reception. Theo's favorite shows included *The Dick Tracy Hour*, *The Adventures of Ozzie and Harriet*, and *The Amazing Nero Wolfe*. Shadow never barked during the radio broadcasts. They were too strange and too absorbing.

Dressed in a white tennis sweater, Jack Adams rang the doorbell of the farmhouse. He was at the official entrance to the house, not the kitchen door. It was Shadow who answered the ring, jumping on the screen, greeting the elderly man with a happy laugh-smile across his face.

When Alice opened the door for Jack, Shadow pushed on the old man's legs, attempting to herd him. When Jack laughed and did not comply, Shadow began to bark. And bark. And bark again. Jack owned Good As New Antiques and was a regular buyer of Alice's landscapes for his store. Alice was flustered with Shadow and sternly commanded him to stop. He did not. Shadow followed Jack into Alice's studio and continued to bark.

"Oh, don't worry about it, Alice," said Jack as he reached down and petted Shadow's head. "He's just a pup. He's just trying to get the old man in line."

That was the beginning of the barking.

Shadow barked when he was hungry, when he was thirsty, and when there was a stranger at the squeaking kitchen door. What was even worse, Shadow was part shepherd. The human farbacks trained his kind to herd, principally sheep and cows. These dogs were generally low to the ground. They butted their noses against ankles and legs, barking too, to keep the cattle together.

Pushing, pushing, pushing the cattle to become a single herd. Nature had room for Shadow's exuberant behavior. But inside the farmhouse, it was a different matter. Shadow continued to gather his flock. He nipped at the heels and ankles of anyone.

Theo had attempted to break Shadow of the habit. He had tried positive reinforcement, which was the training recommended in *The Puppy Book*. Every time Shadow was quiet, he gave him a Cheerio.

Every time he did not push an ankle, he received another Cheerio.

The positive reinforcement did not sink into the canine's mind.

"You've got to try harder, Theo," Alice sternly told him. "Jack Adams has been patient. But today, he called him a nuisance."

Shadow especially liked nipping at Ted's ankles as he passed by. He mischievously wanted the man who always seemed oblivious to him to know that he was the top dog in the farmhouse.

Pushing, pushing, pushing Ted.

"One day, you're going to get it, pooch," Ted said.

Shadow paid no mind. He wanted to make sure everyone understood he was the shepherd. He wanted that to be clear to his master too. *I am top dog. Do you get it?*

When Theo did not walk upstairs to his room like Shadow wanted, the dog would race around Theo and bark at him, signaling him to get upstairs.

Theo stomped his feet. Shadow barked louder. Theo shouted. Shadow barked louder. Theo's face grew red with blood. He pointed a straight finger and proclaimed, "Bad dog! Bad dog!"

Alice saw her husband's attitude rising in the reddening pulse of her son. She thought it would be good if Ahanu Lightstone weighed in on the dog's yapping.

"But why?" asked Theo.

"I want you to be your own man," she replied. "I don't want your nature or your dog to rule you." Alice also wanted quiet in the house. She was an artist and had her portrait work to do, and she certainly did not want to be distracted by him especially when she was with her clients.

At the Monomoy Gas Station, Alice drove the family pickup truck up to the pump. Ted called Shadow a truck-bed dog. He would say "not in the front seat with people. In the truck bed like a dog." Shadow sat in the bed of the vehicle until he saw Ahanu.

Shadow barked loudly, recognizing his friend.

He was so excited, Shadow leapt from the truck. But he did not jump on Ahanu in greeting. Instead, he ran around his jeaned legs, pushing his snout against the man's ankles, barking and yipping, trying to herd the great and towering man-totem.

From the passenger seat, Theo looked at the formidable man in embarrassment. He remembered only too well what the Algonquin had told him. "Master him and in so doing, you shall master yourself."

Ahanu was thrilled to see his Shooting Star. He bent low and hugged the dog who lapped his face. Then he turned to Theo, who flushed with embarrassment. Ahanu understood the shame on the boy's face.

"Theo, my friend," Ahanu said. His face was proud. But his expression was not arrogant. "You have not broken him. You must. You are the alpha, but he thinks he is the alpha. You must show him. He is the guide, but you lead. When you lead and he guides, then you shall walk together."

The Algonquin showed Theo what he must do. He reached across the register in the office. There were several papers left from Sunday. He took the bright comic section from one of the Sunday editions.

"You like the funnies?" Ahanu asked.

"I do," Theo said, looking at the tall station owner.

"Do you like *Blondie, Pogo,* and *Dick Tracy?*"

"I do!"

"What do you like best?"

"I like all of them, sir."

"So," Ahanu said as he took the funnies and rolled them into his hand. "This will not be funny. But it will lead you to fun. You must affect this not with cruelty, but as an act of discipline, for the dog must know you are master."

Then Ahanu instructed him.

Theo did not want to do what Ahanu had suggested. As he rode back to Blueberry Hill with Alice, he looked through the window to the bed of the truck. There was Shadow in the far corner of the bed, thrusting his head upward, letting the air roll over his fur and ears.

"You shall not have to do this more than three times, for Shooting Star is smart, and he is very attached to you."

"You know his name is Shadow, right?" asked Theo.

"He will always be the star to me," Ahanu replied. "You are the leader, Theo. He is but the guide. He knows where the North Star spins, but you must take him there."

Later, on their journey down to the forest bordering the farm, Theo carried the rolled-up funny papers in his back pocket

The wood was a menagerie of blazing red and orange timber—alder, birch, cherry, fir, spruce, and scrub oak.

The boy and dog picked their way through a sprouty bramble of ash and nettles until they reached an old iron gate. There was an aged heraldry of a train locomotive at the top of it—the emblem of the early Snow oligarchy.

"Walk with me, buddy," Theo said. Shadow loyally walked by his side. Through the iron gate, Theo and Shadow strolled in the family cemetery where generations of Snows had been buried. The prayers for the dead seemed to fill the fenced land with a separate peace.

The stones marking the bodies stood up from the ground. Believing the stones were part of a herd, Shadow barked at the gray slabs. When the slabs did not move to come into one solid flock, he barked even louder and crouched, pushing his nose against the headstone as if to herd it.

Dissatisfied with the immovability of the stones, Shadow turned to Theo and started to herd him, yipping at his ankles. Theo did not expect to use the rolled up funny papers on their walk that day, but the opportunity presented itself.

Theo looked down at Shadow. He pulled the roll from his back pocket. Bringing it forward, he snapped the roll onto Shadow's barking snout. Shadow jumped back, his eyes popping wide in shock.

Silence.

For a moment, Shadow watched Theo with astonishment, not comprehending the action. Then, he barked again and came toward Theo's ankles. This time, his barking was more aggressive. Theo rolled the comic section tight and moved toward Shadow's snout. Shadow retreated when he saw the roll.

Theo moved forward. He brought the paper toward the snout. He was surprised to see Shadow open his mouth, baring the fangs of his upper jaw, ready for struggle. Then, for the first time, Theo saw Shadow's lower teeth, also bared, small and childlike. The lower jaw quivered as if the will to aggress was breaking as the dog cried in a shrill scream from the shock that was about to befall him.

Without anger, steady, Theo snapped the paper against the nose of the dog. It was firm but not angry. The howl that came from the dog would suggest otherwise—as if a blade had just cut across his fur. Shadow's eyes went wild with hurt. He withdrew and cowered in the long grass of the cemetery as if he, himself, were dying.

While the boy felt terrible with the feat, he was confounded by Shadow's crying. Before Theo could fully understand, Shadow leapt onto Theo's right leg. Strangely, his paws wrapped around Theo's thigh, and the dog pressed his head against Theo's flesh, prostrate, as if in contrition, laying his head against the boy for what was more than moments.

They walked out of the cemetery together. Shadow was silent all the way back to the farmhouse. For five hours, Shadow hid from Theo. He hid in the farmhouse and on the property. Theo located the dog in the corner of the den behind the sofa. He decided not to say anything.

Later, Theo discovered Shadow in the boiler room lying beneath the oil tank. It was then that Theo instinctively understood Shadow's secret grieving. He was leaving part of his large self behind as he became part of the pack. But he was not the leader of the pack.

Still later, Theo watched as Shadow retreated to the shade beneath the sweetgum tree. Its black-green shade was so dense that the dog could hardly be seen underneath its shadow.

That evening, the dog did not touch his food. As Ahanu suggested, Theo kept the paper rolled up in his back pocket so that Shadow could see it. "You are the leader, not him. He must be able to observe your shepherd's staff, the funny papers, for you are the shepherd, not him."

Shadow slept in his cubby that night while Theo sat on his bed, playing an old set of bagpipes given to him by Cailleach Snow, his grandmother. The bag's fabric was of the Scottish Highlands, for she was a Scotswoman before she became a Snow.

Theo blew into the melody pipe, or *chanter*. The bag and pipes moaned and wheezed. The music sounded as sour and forlorn as Shadow felt. Theo wasn't very good, but he needed to get better. His Boy Scout counselor told him if he could play a tune on the bagpipes, he would be eligible to receive the Bugling merit badge for his sash.

"Grandma says I should learn 'Amazing Grace,'" Theo told Shadow, trying to ignore Shadow's sorrow. "She said that for the rest of my life, I can be a hit at baptisms, weddings, and funerals."

But Shadow wasn't really listening.

He was too busy stewing over the two attacks on his snout to hear Theo's words or observe how awful Theo's pipe-work sounded.

Two weeks later, Shadow attempted one last mastery over the boy.

Pushing, pushing, pushing.

In the woods now stripped of leaves, he barked at Theo. To Theo, it seemed completely random. Shadow stood firm, his back legs flexed commandingly. Shadow barked sharply, proclaiming to Theo he had better get in line.

"No, buddy, I'm the shepherd, and you're my guide." Theo pulled out the paper and smacked him on the snout.

The dog did not recoil nor look astonished. His gaze was not even one of hurt. What Theo saw in his dog's eyes was a new understanding—Theo was the master. Indeed, Shadow acted as if he expected this correction. Instantly, Shadow stopped barking.

When Theo returned to school, and the seventh grade, Shadow missed him but there was Alice. He could run the house, and she would take him out when he needed to. He simply stood patiently by the screen door of the kitchen. The puppy ate twice a day from a silver bowl in the kitchen where there was delicious food and a second silver bowl that always held fresh, cool water. The puppy decided that his mommy was right to sit on her teats and force her boys not to suckle but to eat. *Chicken is tasty!*

Ahanu was right too. It took only three times to break the barking habit. Shadow never ever barked again except when there was danger or in a happy confirmation of joy.

When Jack Adams returned that autumn to fill Good As New Antiques with Alice's paintings, he was greeted by a friendly dog at the door, not a barking one.

And Theo, well, Theo never used the funnies again. One night, Theo took the roll of funnies and, in silent ritual, threw the paper into the fire of the hearth, watching its mass transmute to smoke and embers as if to signal Shadow's passage from pup to dog.

Still, there were times when the hallway rattled, especially in the rooms of that claustrophobic winter where the snowy outdoors did not provide relief from the tensions of life with Ted. When the dog barked at the storms, Theo would bash his palm against the mattress, signaling the dog to leave the cubby and jump up on the bed.

Theo would take him softly in his arms and muzzle him into his chest, so he would not make a sound.

"It's not for us, Shadow," Theo whispered into his ear. "It's not for us."

As hard as it was for Theo, and for the little he could understand it, he obeyed his mother's wishes to stay clear when the crackling zest of the blue electrical storms burned his eyes and ears.

In the morning, when his eyes could see again, Theo pulled his tortoise-shell eyeglasses from the nightstand to carefully investigate the damage of the winter storm.

Theo sometimes found a broken shard of mirror or glass in the hallway that had been missed in the night cleanup. Once, he found a splintered spindle chair from his parent's bedroom. It hid in a snowdrift by the garbage cans outside the barn.

What hurt the boy most was when he found his mother's oil paints trashed, as if the work she did was not valuable to the family and to the farmhouse. Still, like Shadow who had stopped his bark, Theo developed the restraint to not talk about the sad discoveries.

One night, Theo and Shadow huddled together in the bed as a new squall broke. It was spring thaw. When Alice screamed,

Theo's chest puffed forward, a meringue of aggression and fear. Shadow's tail shot upward like a sword unsheathed. Theo jumped from his bed, ran across the room, slammed open the door, and barged into the hallway. Before him was the wide back of his father, granite blue in the stormy light. His father was slapping his mother's face.

"Stop it!" Theo screamed.

His father did not turn but continued to hit his mother. Theo knew there was no appeal against his judgment—only force. Passion is not reasonable. Only the wise know when to stop. His father's neck was thick with rage. The jugular pulsed blue with blood. The muscles in his arms twisted like snakes.

Shadow growled as if he felt the aggressing anger pouring off the man. Theo pivoted. "No, Shadow!"

But Shadow was not about to allow the man to hurt the woman. And no rolled-up paper, even if Theo carried it, was going to stop him from protecting Alice.

Shadow lunged onto the back of Hercules. The dog's paws ripped into the cloth of the shirt. With a horrible-sounding growl, Shadow opened his jaw and bit into Ted's neck to put an end to the angry assault.

Blood smeared Shadow's mouth.

"No, suh!" Ted shouted.

Ted shoved his elbow into Shadow's stomach. The dog fell backward onto the hallway's floor. Ted stood quickly, grabbing his neck with his palm, discovering blood in his hand.

Ted lunged toward Shadow. But as Ted aggressed, Shadow flexed his body in fight. Before Theo could fully comprehend what was happening, Shadow leapt toward the attacker. Ted raised his boot as a shield.

With a furious kick, Ted sent the dog thudding against the wall.

"Damn!" Ted shouted. His face pulsed red with fury. "Keep that dog away from me!"

Ted stuttered, trying to shout again. Then, as if awakening from an astounding nightmare, he surveyed the broken objects of his delirium—his frightened son and his beaten wife. He clamped his mouth in shock and shame. Turning, Ted walked abruptly through the hallway, his boots thundering against the wood.

Theo heard his father's footsteps descend the stairs. The kitchen door squeaked its damnation. Footsteps fell against the driveway. The car door opened. The truck engine wheezed. The wheels ground against the gravel. The truck's sound darkened into lethal silence, descending down the hill of the farm.

Later that night, after he tucked his mother into her bed, Theo did not know what else to do but cry.

He held Shadow close to him. Shadow did not yawn. Shadow did not lick. Shadow was on guard, waiting for the storm to return. Theo did not know what to say to his dog who attacked his father, making him bleed.

He could not say "bad dog."

He could not say "good boy."

He could not say anything.

Quiet breathed like some darkening monster at the window of Theo's mind. In the gruesomeness, he shuddered. Once the exhaustion of his pent-up tension overwhelmed him, Theo fell asleep, holding Shadow against his side. They fell asleep together, close, like potatoes nudged against the Sunday roast.

In the morning, Shadow jumped from the bed. He shook

his body, the head too, rinsing his ears of the dreams of last night's storm. He lowered the front of his golden body and stretched his whole spine like a runner who elongates the calves and thighs before the race. Shadow had grown from the runt of the litter into his maturity. He had the musculature of his adulthood, but the black-and-golden stripes of his youth, the markings of the exotic Bengal tiger, remained. His paws shone clean, like linen, white and textured, against the polished plank of the bedroom floor. He rose from his stretch. His ears jutted upward as Theo spoke to him.

"Let's go outside," said his master. They ran downstairs for the dog's morning constitution.

At the kitchen door, they passed Alice. "Let me take him," she said. And so, Theo did. Alice and Shadow went walking.

As he sat alone, the storm returned.

Theo was at the kitchen table having his cereal when he heard the truck pull up onto the hill. He froze at the sound of it. He heard his father's boots stomp over the gravel and reach the steps to the house. The kitchen door squeaked.

Theo looked up to see his father. "Where's Mother?" he said. Theo observed the wan complexion, the watery-red eyes drowned in the poison of an all-nighter. It did not seem that important for Ted to hide his eyes with his sunglasses. And Theo did not care what repercussions occurred. He *hated* the storm. He despised what it did to his mother, what it did to his family.

"Your wife is out with the dog," Theo finally answered as he turned away from the man and looked into the pitiable last bits of cereal sluicing at the bottom of his breakfast bowl.

"I told you what would happen to that dog if he barked," said the man.

"He would have to sleep in the house behind the barn," said Theo.

"See to it," said the man.

Ted spoke commandingly. He went to the sink, looking for a glass. When he found one, he seemed confused. It appeared he did not know what to pour into it. He turned on the faucet and then turned it off. He picked up the coffee pot. Put it back on the burner.

"See to what?" said Theo with the fighting confidence of rage. "He didn't bark. He *bit* you."

The man placed the empty glass on the counter and gently fingered his neck. He did not seem to want to fight back, lost in his own hurt. The right side of his neck was raised and purple with bruising from the skirmish with Shadow's jaw.

"Did he have his rabies shot?" the man asked. He was suddenly less commanding, his question uttered like a frail child.

"Lucky for you, I lived up to our bargain. Shadow has had all his shots." Ted seem both relieved and angered by his son's admission.

"You never know what a dog is going to get when he's bred in the wigwam of those filthy Indians," Ted said.

Enraged, Theo stood from the table. "Filthy Indians?" he replied with a smirk. "The ones the Snow family stole their land from? Kinda like those dirty Jews that Hitler exterminated? Maybe the army rejected you because you didn't know how to fight for the good guys. Or maybe you have not heard—good guys don't beat women. They don't kick dogs. They don't call people filthy, because they are the good guys." Theo trembled, waiting for his father's attack, wanting it so his mother would not have to suffer.

The man left the sink and came toward the boy.

Theo watched his father's fidget finger twitch nervously in his hand.

Open. Shut. Open. Shut.

"No, suh. No, suh," Ted said.

Yet, Theo had no idea to whom his dad was really talking. Perhaps he was talking to himself?

The man inched closer.

Theo was certain his father was going to whack him.

Then, the muddled clouds of the man's expression seemed to part, and a new sun shined upon him as if he, once again, realized who he was. He smiled.

"Who ever said I was a good guy?" asked the man.

Passing Theo at the table, Ted walked into the hallway, completely ignoring the eyes of his boy as if he were not even there, leaving in his wake the cold government of his machismo.

Chapter Six

Soon the crocuses appeared. Before Theo could blink, there were the daffodils, then the wild irises, and finally the lilies blooming throughout the farmland. "Come on," Shadow said with his whole body. And who could resist such prompting? Theo and Shadow ran through the green, storybook land of spring's Blueberry Hill. Shadow loved this time. Stories were no longer told from books on a bed. He was not Lassie. Nor was he Mighty Dog. He and the boy were *living* the tales as they ran through the long, wild grass.

They lived in morning dreams. In Shadow's imagination, horses became dragons, frogs grew into war tanks, and the distant glasswork smokestacks were the calves and thighs of giants. Theo and Shadow simply needed to slay the dragons before they heard the *clang, clang, clang* of the bell on the hill, signaling that breakfast pancakes were served.

The life inside the farmhouse on Blueberry Hill was less clear.

All the lines appeared crooked, whether winter or spring. The hand at the head of the table that held a palm to pray also held force to ruin. Within the farmhouse, the mistress of the house was compromised.

Outdoors, the woman, well, that was when the woman was queen. When the Bible-black bell on the white beam rang for breakfast, Theo and Shadow would look to the summit from where the bell was tolling.

There stood the benevolent monarch of Blueberry Hill, Alice Snow. She was mother. She was sister. She was love. She stood on the green bosom of her vegetable and flower garden, and Theo and Shadow knew that everything would be well *through her*. They knew this together. They knew this in the blood of their humanity and their animal.

As Shadow was now a year old, he began to walk farther into the world. The clanging of the farm bell would always lead him home, but Shadow had solitary adventures to explore when Theo went to school.

Of course, Shadow bore no leash in his adventures. Shadow did not need it. He was a good, non-barking boy! He knew where the love, warmth, and food could be located. For, at the end of the day, when the sun dropped, what good boy doesn't know how to find his way home?

Shadow strolled down Cockle Cove Road to the place his humans called the "neighborhood." There he found bright painted houses and fences. In the stockaded meadows, there were horses with names such as Galileo, Longfellow, and Cigar. He could not, however, greet them properly since he could not squeeze under the equestrian fences. He admired his fellow mammals from a distance. But even at a distance, he saw the field flies buzzing around Longfellow's ears, worrying his brow. Full of convivial cheer, Shadow barked at the ornery insects, which took flight at the noise. Here, in the neighbor-hood, not in his own home, the grateful horses appreciated such barking.

Shadow loved the delicate affections of the wildflowers. He adored listening to the petals of the bur marigolds and the orange coneflowers trembling in the breeze.

Tall elms towered over the narrow lanes and at the edges of the wide fields in the neighborhood. Cock pheasants strutted in the early greening corn. They stamped their arrowed footprints down into the moist earth. Their scaly toes lifted tiny fragments of soil glittering red in the sunlight.

Beneath the royal-blue sky of the neighborhood, and by a solitary road, Shadow found a secret land known as "the dump" where people would dispose of their garbage and junk.

While this land was reviled by humans, to Shadow it was a magical place of the most succulent fragrances . . . of rotting meat and fermenting apples. He braved the ravaging moths and the mad hornets to romp among the piles of garbage, intoxicated by the smells of life on earth—of brine in the pickling vat, coffee grounds, blackened toast, the flat, moist plug of apple tobacco, decaying books, broken hens' eggs, sawdust shavings, and the whiff of the cold metal in the mattress springs. His nose trembled in the flutter of his nostrils. The odor of metal was so potent he could taste the steel in his mouth.

On his neighborhood walks, Shadow loved bringing his snout low to the mailbox posts and fence poles, so he could discover who had lifted their leg on the territory and who ruled what lands.

The aroma at the Collier fence posts belonged to a brown boxer with an unusually large black snout and charcoal-gray eyes. His name was Zeus. Unlike the Greek god he was named for, Zeus was unsocial and never wanted to play. If Shadow even attempted to place a paw on Zeus's grass or driveway, Zeus would go crazy—howling and yipping, drool falling from his jaw.

Shadow attempted to be neighborly. Zeus wanted none of it. Nevertheless, Shadow learned an important lesson from the old boxer: you avoid squabbles over land when you mark your territory. That way, everyone knows who owns what. Shadow was respectful, as well as scared, of Zeus's growl. So, he did what a good neighbor does; unless invited, he did not stray across the boundaries set by others.

Meanwhile, Shadow spent an entire week executing the unspoken lesson of Zeus. Shadow lifted his leg across his vast account of Blueberry Hill—on stone walls, wheelbarrows, and fence gates so everyone in the distant and abiding lands would know all was under the rule of Shadow.

Of course, this was all part of Shadow's immense imagination. Dogs dream too. And in the dream, his kingdom did not have a patriarch by the name of Ted Snow.

Shadow even had dreams of Cleopatra. She was a long-haired house cat who spent a lot of time in her front yard. She had white fur and yellow paws. When she was curled for sleeping, she had the opalescence of a pearl drop still being refined in the clamshell. Cleopatra liked to lay in the early afternoon sunbeam at the end of her driveway by the mailbox.

Fastidiously licking herself, the cat made sure she was just as tidy as her master's home. She lived in a bright yellow house, extremely shipshape from the outside. In spring and summer, the house held purple lavender in the window boxes. Even in winter, there were snowberries in two earthen pots at either side of the yellow house's red door.

Shadow's dreams of Cleopatra encouraged him. He had high hopes when he first walked over to the strange cat. *After all, why be so neat and lick your paws all day long unless you want to be someone's playmate?*

Shadow was young, but he was not bashful. He was eager

to make allegiances. He had already done that with Cigar and Galileo. When Shadow approached her yard, Cleopatra instantly stood up from her sunbath. Shadow planned to kiss the cat, but she drew her lips back from a set of wicked-looking teeth. Arching her spine and thrusting her puffy white tail straight up into the air, she spat at him. She leveled her sparkling blue Egyptian eyes on him as she batted his nose with her front right paw.

Shadow stopped, puzzled. *Doesn't the white cat want to play?*

The musty fragrance coming from under her tail smelled delicious. Shadow tried to inch in and give Cleopatra's rump a neighborly sniff, but she hissed and spat all the more and raised a paw, nails extended.

Shadow could not help but feel upset. *Okay, I am ready to play with you whenever you want. But I have more important things to care about than a snotty, unneighborly cat.*

If Zeus and Cleopatra don't want to play, Shadow mused, *well, I have my boy.*

And my boy is enough.

That night, Shadow lay against Theo's leg. When he woke, Shadow wanted to get to a warmer place. He inched up on the covers. *Closer, closer.* Up the torso. He pushed his snout to the boy's arm. *Pushing. Pushing. Pushing.* He wanted to burrow into the boy's embrace. Finally, the boy opened his arm away from his chest. Shadow lay his whole head in the crook of his boy's arm. In sleep, Theo petted his dog's head and neck absently, unaware of the creature comfort his dog and he both shared, the belonging to one another in their simple ritual of sleep.

Shadow had never seen anything like it, not even in his dreams. There were chromatic spheres of pink, purple, green, and forget-me-not blue whipping through the air, tethered with leashes much thinner than his. So thin, he could hardly see them. Shadow had heard Alice say it was an important day. This was *the* day Theo became thirteen years old. The balloons heralded the celebration. Half-sized humans, as big or bigger than Theo, in soft pastel dresses and blue-and-white-striped sweaters, scratched, rubbed, and petted Shadow from every point on his vast estate.

Dressed in a button-down checkered shirt and khakis, Ted Snow looked outstanding. His thick brown hair blew in the gentle breeze like a photograph of a dad in *Life* magazine. *On his best behavior*, thought Shadow. Ted even *smiled*.

The half-sized humans grew giddy. The goo of green and purple gummy-bears oozed between their white teeth. They chased one another atop the hill. Screaming. Singing. Their giddiness was infectious. Shadow grew giddy too. For him, everything was as shiny and bright as those colorful spheres riding the indigo sky. A pink balloon popped. Bang! Shadow squashed his eyes. His ears twitched, erect. In their sugar-drenched state of hyper-reality, the children sniggered. They loved Theo's funny, funny dog.

Wafting through the yard outside the kitchen was a most remarkable perfume, even more savory than the fragrances from the dump heaps. His nostrils cinching frantically, Shadow keenly discerned that within the mysterious fragrance was flour, butter, hot milk, eggs, vanilla, and sugar. He had heard that Alice was going to make a hot-milk cake where butter and milk were warmed and ladled into the batter of flour as it was *whipped, whipped, whipped* into the ambrosia fit for the

Greek gods.

The aroma and, then, the realization that the cake was *real* made Shadow even giddier. He definitely wanted to be closer to the cake, to revel in the crisp, warm vanilla that sweetly coursed through summer's air. As half-sized humans came and went through the squeaking screen door to the kitchen, Shadow saw his opportunity to be closer still to the shattering fragrance.

He squeezed past Sally Abernathy and Ben Wheeler as they passed him through the squeaking, open door, making his way into the kitchen.

Oh, the eggs and sugar and vanilla!

Shadow grew sublime, scurrying about the floor, drunk with the aromas emanating from the mixing bowl that Alice whipped at the counter. He drummed his white paws happily into the floor.

"What has gotten into you?" Alice asked with a laugh.

Shadow's red tongue lollygagged about his mouth as he trembled in manic anticipation.

Oh, the hot butter! Oh, the hot milk!

At the counter, Alice picked up the silver bowl filled with that magic concoction she called "frosting" and walked to the harvest table in the middle of the kitchen. Her shiny church shoes, black patent leather, clattered across the polished planked floor. Her crinoline petticoat rustled beneath her dress. In perfect synchronicity, Shadow moved his shoulders and flanks to her lovely, feminine sashay.

Now, he sat at his queen's feet, next to her table, watching every move tremulously. There, she iced the towering hot-milk cake with the sweet white frosting. In awe, Shadow watched as Alice, with a spatula, wrapped the white alchemy around the milk cake. It hung on the cake like the magic mist at first light surrounding Blueberry Hill. The sugary redolence climbed up his nostrils like the smoky hands of a genie, twisting down his throat, throttling his heart in an enchantment.

"I really shouldn't, but it's a special day, Shadow. So why not?" said Alice with a smile.

Indeed, why not? Shadow thought.

He whimpered in desire. He ran in place, his linen-white paws thudding against the wood planks of the kitchen floor.

"Our boy is becoming a man. Thirteen. Can you believe it, Shadow? Thirteen. In just a few years, he'll be driving!" She leaned down and patted him, bringing the wooden mixing spoon to his mouth. *It is just like the wooden spoon that my boy fed me with when I was but a pup! My spoon! My frosting!* But this time, his spoon was not covered with mouth-watering peanut butter but with sparkles of pink and white sugar! *Waaaaaa!* The spoon nudged his mouth. *Now, take it!* He licked and lolled and swooned around that spoon with his entire blithering tongue.

He was dizzy with pleasure. What he had smelled in the yard had materialized as real food in his mouth. *It is more delightful than a dream, this wondrous frosting!* Alice patted his head, saying "What a good boy you are!"

I am a good boy, Shadow thought, thrilled with the smell and taste of *my special cake for the boy's special day. I am a good boy, so why should I not enjoy my cake right now?*

As Alice moved to the sink to rinse the mixing bowl and utensils, Shadow saw his destiny awaiting him.

I could float. No table or balloons in the sky can stop me now. I serve Superman! I have a cape too, and I can fly! I am flying! I am Mighty Dog!

Shadow shoved his whole mouth and nose into the good-boy cake. Soon, his entire head plunged into paradise. He smelled the delight of butter and sugar and peppermint and vanilla and cinnamon and milk as his mouth sucked in the moist density of the cake. He gushed with pleasure as the wonder-cake tumbled into his tummy.

Alice screamed.

Shadow turned. He stood on all fours on top of the harvest table.

How did I even get here?!

He signaled to Alice, lifting his big brown eyes, upward in a dog smile.

Nothing to worry about, Mom.

All is fine with your good boy.

Thank you for this delicious cake!

Happy, happy birthday to us all!

"No, Shadow! No. Bad dog!" she replied. "Bad dog! Bad dog!"

The screen door burst open, and there was Ted, his face ruddy, his mouth set with clenched teeth. He marched straight for the table while the kitchen door screeched.

"Get off!" Ted shouted. He grabbed Shadow by his collar. Yanking at it, he threw Shadow off the table and to the wooden-planked floor. The stainless-steel water bowl spilled. Church shoes clattered. The petticoat rustled. The man kicked Shadow's hinders with his right boot as the dog cowered and whimpered.

"Bad dog!" Ted shouted. "Bad dog!"

Ted dragged the whimpering creature across the floor and shoved him through the gap in the screen door. In their pink party dresses and white button-down collars, the half-sized humans on the hill laughed. They glanced at Shadow's ears and snout covered in a white mash of frosting and cake. They sniggered more.

They loved Theo's funny, funny dog.

"Uh oh!" cried Sally Abernathy, followed by a giggle.

As Ted dragged the dog down the concrete steps and through the yard, Theo ran toward Shadow.

CHAPTER SEVEN

"Where are you going?" asked Theo. Ted dragged Shadow away from the house.

"Where do you think I'm going?" the patriarch said in a low growl.

As Shadow yelped, Ted lugged him toward the field beyond the driveway.

Shadow tried to stand and walk with Ted, but Ted moved his big plowman's body so quickly it was impossible for Shadow to rise into a walking position. The dog's attempt to gain ground only made it worse as he struggled on the gravel driveway. Ted's frame tilted against the weight of the dog. The friction of the sharp stones rubbed the fur on Shadow's rump clean. By the time the dog reached the back of the barn, his haunches were raw and bleeding.

"No, Dad. Stop it!" Theo cried.

"It's staying here," replied Hercules.

Ted found the iron post next to the dog shelter. "Many a Snow dog has lived here. That's the problem with this dog. It thinks it's one of us. It's a dog, Theo! It's a dog! Dogs belong in the yards, not in our homes!"

"He's bleeding!" Theo said as he looked at the back of Shadow, who grappled to reach his raw shanks to lick them.

Ted yanked the collar at Shadow's neck with such fury, the dog yowled. Shadow lunged at Ted. His lips curled. His pink gums rose aggressively. His fangs shone. In an instant, the long fingers of Ted's big hand closed into the fist of his patriarchal privilege. It moved with the quivering intensity of a hunter's arrow. In that instant, there was nothing swifter. Nothing more powerful. Ted slammed his fist into Shadow's head.

"Stop it, damn dog, or I'll kill yuh!" Ted shouted.

"No! Dad!" Theo cried as he ran toward Shadow, who lay flattened on the ground next to the chain post. The boy fell to the ground, touching the crown of Shadow's head.

The dog looked at Theo. *I am fine. Don't worry.*

"Leave him be!" the father said. He grabbed Theo at the nape of his blue-and-white-striped sweater. He shoved him back toward the house and the party.

As he was dragged away, Theo howled as if he would never see his dog again.

Shadow returned the boy's heartbreak with his yowl.

The hamburgers and hotdogs were served. As planned, the party went on. The children sat at five different picnic tables, laughing and telling stories. Many had second helpings of burgers and dogs. Some had thirds.

Alice brought a fresh water bowl to Shadow. The dog sat.

He drank the water. Theo Snow smiled and talked with his friends, but he was feeling Shadow, enslaved at the back of the barn. Theo's friends had come to celebrate him. Alice told him that he could not let them down. As best he could, the boy pasted a happy look on his face, aching uncontrollably inside. He watched his father, the barnacle-breasted Neptune, eat silently at the table, his hamburger thick with mayonnaise.

Summoned by a plea for a replacement birthday cake, Lynette Magruder from the local bakery, in her 1944 red Ford, drove up the driveway to the Snow farmhouse. Lynette was a robust woman, her skin like poultry. She carried two boxes filled with twenty-four cupcakes and marched right into the kitchen.

"The cavalry is here!" she announced in her peppery voice.

After lunch, Theo quietly slipped into the kitchen. He filled another water bowl for Shadow. He carried it out to the yard. But his father's power hand, his right hand, was on him. He yanked the bowl from Theo's hands. The fresh water splattered onto the grass.

"Mrs. Lightstone said dogs should always have water!" Theo shouted.

"He'll have it soon enough," said Ted as he looked up at the sky.

Black rain clouds rolled over the vaulted heavens. Storm air filled Theo's nostrils. The clouds' shadows crawled over the blackening heads of the clover. The thunder boomed like a celebration drum.

Gada. Gada. Gada.

Every rhythm prepares a future.

Alice and Lynette Magruder carried two trays of cupcakes

out from the kitchen. Thirteen small cakes were lit with blue candles.

The two trays arrived at the birthday boy's bench where, after the obligatory birthday song, Theo quickly blew them out. A large hurrah lifted in rebellion against the darkening day.

In reply, the atmosphere flashed blue lightning. The sky thundered.

Gada. Gada. Gada.

The sounds were as profound as the thumping over the Lost Boys from Ahanu's drum from so many seasons past.

At Alice Snow's prompt, the children, carrying their cakes and plates, ran into the house as the raindrops began to fall. Around the gaily wrapped birthday presents, Ted hoisted the corners of the red-and-white-checked tablecloth. Then he pulled the gifts from the table in one move. Like a dangerous Santa Claus, Ted carried the birthday boon into the house.

The downpour unleashed itself as Theo absently opened his presents in the living room with the other children. He did his best to be of grateful spirit, but his heart remained chained to his dog.

The storm was powerful. It pelted the roof and the ground with force. A bew of partridges raced into the wood for cover. In Theo's mind, the desperate images of Shadow grew so persuasive that Theo couldn't do anything but sneak out of the party, put on his jacket, and go to him. But Ted was there at the door to block him.

"That dog needs to learn a lesson," said Ted. "This rain won't hurt him."

"He didn't know, Dad. I am sure he thought the cake was for him."

"That's the problem, Theo. A dog doesn't know. *We know.* Shadow's just an animal."

"*Not just*, Dad. Not *just an animal*," Theo said. "He was once a wolf!"

"There you go again, speaking like a dirty injun!"

The cold rain continued all day in abrading thunder and flaring lightning. In late afternoon, the cars and trucks came to take the young party guests home. Under the rapid assault of the raindrops, black umbrellas opened, flying from car door to kitchen door and back again, closing, lending a pattering death knell to what seemed to Theo like funereal proceedings.

With the last of the children gone, Theo rushed to his mother in the kitchen. Fear etched her brow as Ted's feet beat in a pace on the floor above them.

"I have to get the dog out of the rain," Theo said, anguished.

"I know. I know," she said, her eyes lifting to the gathering storm in her own bedroom. The pacing on the wooden floor above was palpable. "Be patient. Keep quiet. Wait . . ."

"He's not leaving."

She listened. The rhythm in the walking above them shifted. Then, for a moment, the pacing stopped altogether.

"He's just about to," she said.

Theo decided not to question his mother's discernment. She was his champion. Just as importantly, she knew what made the winds of the dragoon blow and recede.

Alice motioned her son into the small living room to shift the atmosphere away from the doomed sounds of the kitchen ceiling. She knew the trigger points of her husband. If she could just keep herself and Theo calm for a short while, Ted would, indeed, leave. Then, Theo could bring Shadow to relative safety in the barn. By the time Ted returned home, he would be looking for nothing but his pillow to sleep off his jag.

To keep him occupied, Alice asked Theo to light a fire in the hearth. Theo stacked the wood, crushed the newspaper to get the flames started, and lit the fire.

When Alice was young, she had no idea what a jag even was. In those early days of their love affair, Alice found Ted's rogue demeanor attractive. He was a Snow. But he was a rebel. He stood up to his stern father, and *no one* in the Snow family did that. The Snows were all too afraid of losing their entitlements. Ted had a relaxed swagger in his walk. Alice loved his confidence, the fashion of his easy laughter. She had no idea, not even a suspicion, that it was drink that fueled his swagger as well as his gumption. He was almost always drunk. But she was a teenager and a dreamer, and she loved his seeming fearlessness. He was handsome as well, with soft eyes that had a happy mischief to them. His thick, curly hair bounced as he swaggered. He was a picture. She thought he was hardy and strong, but it was the heat of the alcohol that made his cheeks flush apple red. He appeared to be the picture of health, but indeed, he wasn't. He never was.

As Alice sat on the sofa, Theo pulled out a thick Highland plaid from the afghan chest. He opened it for Alice, covering her body from the chill of the storm. She thought about how the best thing in her life was her son. Now, she just wanted to protect him from being bruised by the anger of his father.

Alice asked Theo to sort out his birthday toys while they both waited, in collusion, for Ted to leave the house. He sat on the floor and stacked his presents into categories. He had five new hardcover books and seven new Supermans. Theo was thirteen, coming into the age of his teenage years. After the incident with the birthday cake and the violence Ted had demonstrated against Shadow, Alice had walked upstairs and phoned her mother in Boston. Next week, she and Theo and Shadow were going to live with her.

As the night set in, Alice looked at the curtains that framed the picture window. They glistened from the light of the hearth flames. But not even the warm fire could calm her. She was racked with species shame—by the cruelty men showed to Indians, to wives, and to animals.

Over a year ago, Alice had stood on the bluff above the ocean. She saw a man and dog running in the tide, happy, caught in the moment.

The reddish, long-haired dog, spotting Alice, ran to her, shaking the ocean from his fur, wagging his tail. He was so friendly. As she kneeled to pet the dog, a man came to get him, apologizing. He explained that he was training him to run off leash but the dog, "didn't yet have the hang of it."

"No need to apologize," Alice said, laughing.

As they talked, Alice saw Ted in the man. The man was soon to be married. He laughed easily. He was considerate. There was such youthful hope in him . . . and kindness. But this man was a wholesome Ted. A Ted without demons or deceptions, unbroken by the cruelty of a stern, officious father.

The man told Alice that he had grown up with dogs. That he was "a dog guy."

Soon after, Alice had the notion that Theo should have a dog. Perhaps a dog would help him through adolescence, to be a better man like the sweet man at the beach.

As she sat on the sofa, she loved the way Theo had grown in responsibility and in compassion by having a dog. Because of Shadow, Theo even spoke of becoming a veterinarian. She loved that idea too. She felt the decision to find a dog for him had been a wise one. With fancy, she often thought her encounter with the man on the beach had been more than a coincidence. It was as if he were an angel. He had come to deliver a message of hope—the dog. Yet, her grasp was slipping. She could not control Ted except by tiptoeing around him. Now, she could not abide his heartlessness to the dog.

At the sound of descending footsteps on the stairway, Alice turned to Theo sitting on the floor. He heard the footfalls too. Alice caught his glance.

Lightning's forks filled the window frame in the living room. The slamming of the truck door brought Theo to his feet. From the window, Theo watched Ted's truck pull out from the hill. The world was growing darker with nightfall. The truck's headlights beamed. A mangy red fox flashed across the drive-way.

With his father gone, it was time to act.

"I'll put him in the barn," Theo said. "I can dry him off there. I've packed some iodine and some bandages for his haunch-es. I may be a while," Theo said.

"I understand," Alice replied. In her eyes, Theo could tell she was proud of him.

Alice rose from the sofa. She walked over to the electrical switches by the doorway. "There, I've got the floodlights for you."

In the kitchen, Theo put on his yellow rain gear and braced himself against the deluge of rain. Underneath his slicker, he packed Shadow's kibble, bandages, and medicines inside a paper lunch bag.

Like a hammer's head, rain bludgeoned Theo as he dashed down the kitchen steps, across the hummock, and toward the barn. He ran through the slippery grass. The slickness overtook him. He teetered on one foot and fell into the muddy gravel of the driveway. His glasses flew from his face. The dog's kibble crunched against his stomach. He lurched upward so the kibble would not get wet.

"I'm coming, Shadow," he shouted as he rummaged in the puddles for his lost glasses. But it was useless in the dark. Hardly able to see without his prescription, he headed to the barn.

The cold rain continued to pummel him, hitting his yellow slicker, reverberating against his skin. He ran beneath the roof of the barn where a slim edge of eaves protected him from the eager storm. He inched along the red walls to the back of the barn where the steel post tethered the dog.

"I'm almost there, Shadow!" he cried. But there was no scurrying of paws against the ground. There was no bark. Nothing seemed alive.

"Shadow?" Theo said softly. There was no answer.

Without his glasses, the panicked Theo could see little, but he could make out the post, dull and desolate in the dark-green, watery night.

Theo grabbed the lone steel chain at the post and drew it through his hands. Against the driving rain, he looked into his palms. The collar was there. It had been chewed open, and Shadow was gone.

A deep dread settled into Theo's stomach. Theo had nothing but his voice and his legs.

"Shadow!" He screamed into the thrashing rain. Louder and louder he shouted. The dog knew Theo's voice, and if Shadow heard it, Theo was certain Shadow would come running. But he was nowhere in the green obscura.

"Shadow!" Theo shouted.

Through the yellow fog of the floodlights, a ghostly form loped out of the dark ridge of forest. The head was bent, the gaze fixed on the ground. Theo reached out to the soaked form. Shadow brushed up against Theo. Theo knelt down and hugged the wounded animal. But Theo did not experience relief—simply an added strain to make things right for his dog.

"Come on, boy, let's get you warm."

Inside the house, Theo and Alice cleaned the dog's chaffed haunches with soap, warm water, and mercurochrome. Alice dried Shadow with the hot blow of her Handy Hannah Hair Dryer.

In the kitchen bathroom, Theo could not help but sense that Shadow was guarded. He had suffered the blows of his father. He had eaten his way through his collar. Now he was back home, yet Shadow would not look at Theo.

But for the battering rain, the house was quiet. Theo heated up some chili while Alice, curled on the sofa, read *For Whom the Bell Tolls*. Before the fire, Shadow played with the many Supermans that were stacked on the floor. His rump was wrapped in salve and a white cotton bandage. The kitchen steamed from the heat of the house, so Theo cracked open the door to let in the air.

Lulled by the repetitive raindrops, Alice had fallen asleep. She awakened when she heard Ted shouting. "What is wrong with you! Drop it! Drop it now!" But it was not Ted. It was Theo.

Alice blinked. Theo, red-faced, his fists clenched, towered over the dog. Shadow had chewed the Supermans on the floor. They lay disfigured on the rug. He had one in his jaw, so mangled it looked like a chew bone. Theo yanked at the toy in Shadow's mouth. But the dog would not let go. While Theo pulled on it, Shadow dug his paws into the floor. "First the cake, then my dad, and now my Supermans!" Theo shouted. "You ruined the party! You are a bad dog. Bad dog!"

"What has gotten into you?" Alice said as she stood from the sofa. "Stop it. Shadow's upset!"

"He messed with my stuff," Theo shouted. Alice saw the anger leap across his face. She could hardly believe her eyes.

"It's just stuff!" she shouted.

"MY stuff!"

Alice looked at Shadow. He was cowering on the floor, his eyes dimmed in fear. He looked so hurt, she thought he might just die.

"Look at him! The poor guy's been through so much!" She leaned over, petting Shadow's starry crown. He flinched at her touch. "He's been hurt!"

"You'll be a lot more hurt if you don't get out of here, you damned dog!"

Shadow yelped.

Theo raised his foot in a threat to kick him. As if he couldn't see anything but attackers at both flanks, Shadow's face dimmed further. From his crouch, he scampered, running into the kitchen.

Theo gripped his fists tighter. Alice grabbed him with both

hands. "Listen to me! You're hurt too! You're hurt too, Theo! But you have to learn to live with it. You can't take it out on the ones you love."

"But Shadow messed up my stuff!"

"Because he's upset! Can't you understand? Be him for a minute. He's dragged across the driveway. He's chained to a post. For all he knows, he was left there to die! He's not a burden, Theo. You love him. You must show him that love."

"But why would he do what he did?" Theo said as he looked at the damage around him.

"Because he's angry or he's lost," Alice replied.

It was then that Theo understood. His mother was right. What was the one thing she was always trying to teach him? Kindness.

He went into the kitchen. The wind blew at his face. The door was wide open. Shadow was gone. Just a few hours ago, Theo had witnessed a miracle—his dog had chewed through his collar but was still in the woods. Now, that miracle had slipped from his grasp like sand through his fingers.

Theo grabbed his raincoat and slipped into his waders. He ran outside, closing the door behind him. Alice knew there was no stopping him. Not after what she had just said. She looked at the rain puddled on the wooden floor. Praying for deliverance for her son and his dog, she grabbed a mop and pail from the mudroom closet. She mopped up the rain.

CHAPTER EIGHT

"Walk with me!" Theo screamed out to the deluge. In the glossy grass, he struggled to the farm bell. He pulled on the wet gray rope. With all the muscles of his shoulders, he yanked on the cord again and again and again.

The bell's clang was muted in the colossal downpour.

This time, there was no answer.

He did not know what to do but to run the familiar roads Shadow and he traveled on their walks each day. Crackling lightning lit the way. Theo did his best to run Cockle Cove Road, shouting out for his dog in the formless night. Shadow had run away, but a piece of Theo went with him. He could feel him. Tears streamed, running like a hot river down his rain splattered face.

Theo raced the dirt paths between the long sea grass. He shouted everywhere—out to the familiar places his dog knew.

"Shadow! Walk with me!" He screamed. "Walk with me, buddy!"

Shadow had reached the ocean. The storm had pulled the tide high. The yellow air was loaded with mist. For Shadow, the specter of the entire world had grown golden. He heard the mist in the storm call his name.

Bad dog! Bad dog!

That was not your cake!

Get out of here, you damned dog!

Bad dog! Bad dog, Shadow!

The storm was more than dreadful. It was nothing. Even the shape of Thunderbird could not be seen in the overpowering void. He was alone but for his own wooly stink. For all Shadow tried to be to the boy, even the boy had turned against him, growing into another dragoon that thumped through the house.

The blood in his veins beat inside his ears. Wanting to die, Shadow paddled into the bitter sea, yearning to return to the characterless brume that was all around him, the stuff of existence before the light of life.

As he swam into the waters, the dog felt the thrumming rain on the top of his skull. It gave some sort of face to the cipher.

"No, no," howled Shadow. "Do not keep me here!"

"Do you not love the boy?" said the voice of the sea.

"Love is terrible!" Shadow howled.

"I know," replied the sea.

"It is full of hurt."

"It is. But do you not love the boy?"

"I do love the boy!" the dog cried.

"There are many storms, my love," the sea whispered. The voice shook the void. The voice grew warmer. It became the voice of Shadow's mother. A golden imminence rose from the abyss of the sea, striped in the black of the night and the gold of the mist like a Bengal tiger. Ascending, the Great Mother looked from the sea. Two spheres rose, forming a pair of blazing-lantern eyes. When their flames caught the gaze of her beloved son below, they flared with urgency.

Then, suddenly, a great awe fell upon Shadow. It was an awe that turned his muscles to water. It was an awe that smote. The vision held him and possessed him utterly.

"You cannot leave the boy in this storm, not if you truly love him," she said. Her flaring eyes grew kind as she lowered her head toward him. "In your deepest heart, you know you cannot retreat. Theo understands the language of the wind. He will bring the message of the animal to the people. Why did I stir the Lightstones to give you to him? I knew you could guide him. I trusted you. This is part of the great adventure I promised you. Was I wrong to put my faith in you, my son, when you were so small? This is not your time to die. Your sacrifice is yet to be. The boy must learn that fairness is not the full truth. The truth lies in the rightness of all things for that is where peace lives. Only you, Shadow, can take him to that land."

The galling weight of the tide bore it all away. Overwhelmed by it, in that moment, Shadow forgot that he had ever been born. He beheld the fire in the rainy eyes of the night. He heard the music of the spheres. As the tide ebbed, Shadow returned to the shoreline at the ridge of the immeasurably deep ocean.

Twisting, a fissure emerged in the murk. The sun shone through a hole in the cider sky, brightening a funnel of seeing. Never had Shadow noticed the sand so luminous, the green sea grass so vivid, Red, the cedar tree, so large and pervasive.

"I have opened the eye of the storm for you," the Great Mother said. "Run through, my love, before it closes!"

In the utter clearness, Shadow grappled upward from the sand. It would only be a short time until the eye turned and the velocity of the storm returned.

While he had never experienced the eye of a storm first hand, Shadow had a knowledge of it. It was written in the marrow of his bones by all the dogs and wolves who had come before him. He raced through the funnel of momentary serenity.

He knew how he could find his way into the town. If he could get to town before the storm returned, he knew he would be safe until he could find his way home. Even Mother Earth was on his side. *I am not a bad dog, after all. I am a good boy. And don't all good boys find their way home?*

As Theo sprinted down Cockle Cove Road into town, he remembered the miles he and his dog had run since spring had come. As he looked at the road in front of him, it was opaque—a blur of dark black-green. The eye of the storm had passed; the downpour was, once again, oppressive.

He was living inside the brush stroke of one of his mother's paintings—lending definition in his movement to a dark color he could not fully see.

The racing exhausted him, but his spirit was strong. "Shadow," he cried. He ran past the Mayflower Hotel on the edge of town.

He needed to check the sidewalk of Kresge's, Saywells, the front steps of the Congregational church, and the library porch—all places that Shadow knew from the outside.

There was nothing but water pooling outside Kresge's. There was nothing at the church but two lamps burning at either side of the double doors.

Theo passed the wooden sign of the Windjammer. As angry as Theo was with his father, he braved the door, swinging it open.

A purple-neon fish swam over the shanty-style bar. The silhouette of the bartender looked through the purple-gray mist. Theo flexed his eyelids against the haze to see the bartender.

"By the look of you, you must be Ted Snow's kid," the bartender said.

"I am," Theo said. Even in the mania of the storm, he was embarrassed to admit it.

"Your dad's out looking for the dog. Your mom called ten minutes ago."

"Thank you, sir," Theo said as he swung the door closed.

"Be careful out there!" the bartender shouted.

Theo's next stop was the public library. Theo looked through the raging winds and across the murky town square. Even without his glasses, he spied the white building in the distance. It seemed to be awash with hard, unnatural light.

He ran toward it.

As he sped through the lashing rain, Theo observed that the porch of the library was bright with light.

Two lamps from a parked pickup truck appeared to be lighting the library porch. With his weak eyes, Theo could not see more than that. Still, the light was enough for him to race toward the misty destination.

As Theo grew closer, something moved. Two figures sat at the top of the steps to the porch, cut by the bright headlights of the parked truck. Coming closer still, Theo saw that it was his father and Shadow sitting beneath the roof of the porch.

"He's alright," his father called out. "Just shaken and wet."

Theo cried out to the dog. The dog looked up and saw his life in front of him. *The boy. The storyteller. The encourager. My highest allegiance.*

Shadow leapt up, his tail wagging above his bandaged rump in the disordering rain. His back and mid-section were covered in a red Woolrich blanket. Ted held the end of Shadow's new collar so Shadow would not bolt.

Theo rushed to his dog on the porch. He grabbed him into his arms and wept. The wooly stink of him never smelled so good. His father spoke slowly. "Amos Nelson opened Kresge's," Ted said. "He gave these to me in case I found your dog."

Theo was drained, guilty, relieved, happy, and terrified. Even in his current state, he sensed the rum on his father's breath. He gulped back his tears, for he knew his father sat in cold judgment of such emotion.

"Yuh. Big boys of thirteen don't cry," said his father as he stood on the porch. "Let's go home."

Theo felt small against the bleak surmise of his father.

But, his dog was found. *Shadow's alive!* The boy then stood and walked Shadow by the leash to the bed of the truck.

"Let him come up front with us. It's cold and wet in the

truck bed," said Ted, his own checkered shirt flat and wet against his chest and belly.

Theo guided the dog to the front seat. Shadow had never sat in the front of the truck.

It is often said the obliviousness of children, of Nature, of dogs, saves us. Such was this night. Theo sat next to Shadow, wrapped in the red woolen warmth of the Woolrich blanket, holding him tightly. In his blindness, Theo felt fused with the whole world.

Ted turned over the engine. It wheezed. He ground the gears, moving the truck through the deluge.

"I still don't like him. But you do," his father said.

They drove through the small town. Theo could see little through the windshield, but his senses were alive.

The three of them—the beater, the boy, and the dog—said nothing all the way home, anchored in the weight of their terrible love.

CHAPTER NINE

In the downstairs bathroom, Theo put a dry set of bandages on Shadow's rump. Even in his pain, Shadow hung his head in disgrace. He would not look at Theo. Shadow knew he had done wrong by running away. As for Theo, he, too, was shamed by his own angry tirade over his Supermans.

With both hands, the boy lifted the dog's head upward to his own eyes. Fondly, he looked for forgiveness from his dog. Even then, with Theo staring tenderly at him, Shadow glanced away from his master's eyes. Finally, in a strange, stuttering movement, Shadow raised his weakened left paw. The dog held up the paw until Theo reached for it.

Theo shook the paw. The paw and hand remained conjoined, suspended together in mid-air, as if to say, *all of this was wrong, all of it, but still we are friends, forever.*

Theo felt something strange that night—a part of him slipping away. That part where everything had boundaries. He liked to put everything he knew in a category. The kids at school called him a "stickler." The broccoli on the plate could not touch the beef. The cats could not be kept with the dogs. He was Theo, not Ted. Mom was mom *for him.* But Mom was not mother *for Ted.* He let the stickler part of him fall away.

He let the night bore it all away. Perhaps, life was not so cut and dry. There was night and day, but there was twilight too. There was good and bad, but there was forgiveness too. He was definitely going to try harder with his dad, with Alice, and with Shadow. There was only one thing. About the animals. Animals were he and she. Animals were not it. He could never let his dad get away with that.

"The radio is calling it a hurricane. Hurricane Sally. I don't know why they are always using women's names. We never raise hell," Alice Snow said to Theo. Then she winked. He sat at the kitchen table spooning his morning cereal. Shadow was sitting by his side, his haunches and rear still in the bandages. "No damage to town but for a few fallen trees and telephone lines," Alice said as if she were reciting the storm report.

"And those glasses of yours," she said. She placed the cracked frames and lenses on the napkin next to Theo. "Found them this morning in a puddle on the driveway. I suppose you will have to go on seeing without your eyes for a few more days."

Theo studied his spectacles. Both lenses were cracked. He pulled one of them from the frame. It held together like the shattered ice on a skating pond.

This was big trouble for him.

Slowly, Theo looked up to his mother's face to register her level of darkness. She was close enough for him to see.

The darkness simply was not there. All he could see was her sweet, liquid eyes and her proud New England chin. She seemed almost cheerful. "It was an accident," she said. Her brow showed no tension.

"I'll order a new set today, but it will take a while. The lenses are made in Boston."

Ted Snow seldom ate breakfast with the family. This morning, he came down the stairs and sat at the table. Theo thought it strange, for as soon as his father settled in the chair, Alice brought him a mug and poured hot steaming coffee into it. They said nothing because, to Theo, it seemed that somehow everything between them had already been said.

He blinked. *What happened? They are together.*

"Mornin', Theo," Ted said. It was so unlike him to say anything.

"Mornin', Dad," Theo replied.

Alice brought over the cream and sugar bowls from the counter. She placed them by Ted's cup.

"Your father has something to say to you," said Alice. Theo watched as Alice's hand moved across the table and pressed against Ted's open hand. His father took it. Theo was surprised. Something had happened. She held his hand in encouragement. Perhaps, even in love.

Theo looked at his father.

"I am sorry, son. I am going to get help."

Then Theo, on the verge of tears, said, "I'm going to try harder too." He did not know why he was going to cry. He was simply exhausted. Exhausted being the arrogant, smart aleck tough guy to his dad's brutality. Maybe if he really tried and his dad really tried, perhaps, at last, they could be father and son. Theo liked the idea. Then it didn't matter whether it was Ted or Theodore or Ted Jr. or Ted II or anything at all. What's in a name? There would be nothing in a name. Then, the four of them would simply be family. He liked that idea even better.

Much happened in the two weeks it took for Theo to get his new prescriptions from the Dairilee Laboratory in Boston. Life is like that. Some days never seem to end. Nor does anything ever seem to occur. Then whoosh! The dew falls. The owls hunt. The sun burns. Everything is happening. What should have taken months, or even years, sometimes transpires almost overnight. Following the hurricane, the earth steamed. The smells of the land rose up, and Shadow chased the fragrances throughout the hill.

   In those fifteen days without his glasses, Theo started his summer job—painting the farmhouse. The farm had been in the Snow family for centuries, and every ten years or so, as his mother had told him, it needed a fresh coat of paint. Theo was to finish painting by the end of August before school started.

   Since he could see objects close to him without his glasses, he had no trouble painting clapboard from a few inches away, whether on the high ladder or on the ground. He completed the blue trim of the window sills and the eaves as he went along. This broke the monotony of his job and made it more interesting. The trim had always been blue just as it seemed that the hill had always been called Blueberry. Theo avoided painting near the sweetgum tree that stood outside his window. Its spiky fruits, known as gumballs, fell from its star-shaped leaves, thumping onto the ground all around him. There was too much chaos near the tree right now. As gumballs were a favorite food of squirrels and chipmunks, Shadow was busy chasing the little beasts from the house. Theo would wait on that area of the house until all the gumballs had fallen.

   When not chasing, the dog dutifully did his work by laying his body against the lowest rung of the ladder, keeping Theo steady as he painted the second-story clapboards.

Without clear sight, the world was formless for Theo, filled with splotches of color and shade, like the dabbed paints on his mother's mixing palette.

Except the colors moved. They were alive.

His hearing grew more acute, like a dog's. He listened to the birdsong, the wind shifts, and the drifting music from tinny car radios and erratic ice cream trucks on the distant roads.

His nose grew more sensitive too. Just like a dog's. There was the luscious smell of barbecue smoke. The scent of his mother's expensive perfume from France, *Chanel No. 5*. The fecund fragrance of the vegetable garden after a summer shower. He was forged with the heightened sensate of his dog. The great New England naturalist Henry David Thoreau wrote, "It often happens that a man is more humanely related to a cat or a dog than to any human being." The bond between Theo and Shadow had deepened. There was nothing that was such a salve to a boy's grieving heart than a dog returning, especially a dog returning from a fierce, uncertain storm and his once angry owner. *It's just like Lassie*, Theo mused brightly, *when she came home to Joe Carraclough*. But, unlike Joe, Theo had grown angry with his dog and raised his foot to kick him. "I will never ever raise a hand to you, boy," Theo promised. "Never again."

In the evening before dinner, Theo Snow would cool off by diving into the lake at the bottom of the hill. If no one was near, he would skinny-dip. In its depths, the pools within the lake were blue and lucid. Shadow would watch on the bank or sometimes join Theo in the swim. In those liquid times, as he swam in the middle of the lake, Theo heard the birds sing. He smelled the salt water of the outlying ocean. On the lake shore, he would lie on a bath towel and let the falling sun dry the water from his naked body. Shadow lay on his back like an upturned table, the way he always liked to lay, his four white paws in the air. As the water evaporated in his pores, Theo felt connected to the vast immensity some called God.

Shadow's stomach growled.

"Animals," said Theo in delight. His eyes traveled skyward to the red sunset of summer. "Just a couple of animals, we are." Theo laughed.

The dog barked, but he barked in joy.

That summer, Theo slept at night in his twin bed with Shadow lying flat-pressed against his leg or against his back, like the dog packs of old. And all of it seemed to be inter-connected through one grand brushstroke of existence. Nothing was too near or too far. In the circadian cycle, there was balance and routine. To Theo, all of life was one—an immense pouring-out in one beautiful continuum. From his high ladder, Theo watched the cloud of farmers work the low blue swath of berry across the fields. It was the summer of the cicadas. Their timbal organs flicked like light switches, their rhythmic sound covering the hill as Theo painted.

He observed his father, a daub of flesh and white, streak through the pewter-colored twilight. At dusk, back from the Snow Glassworks, his father ran laps around the wood-laden parameters of the property. Theo was proud of his father. He had replaced his nightly ruins at the Windjammer with runs around the farm. It was not long before Theo witnessed a brushstroke of golden voltage at the side of his father's pacing daub. The gold was as undeniable as the fawn's fur from N. C. Wyeth's illustrations in one of Theo and Shadow's favorite books, *The Yearling*.

It was Shadow running at his father's side.

When did they bury the hatchet? When I wasn't looking,

Theo mused, laughing. He was glad for it. But that was the way of Shadow and almost all dogs. Shadow, like all the others in his tribe, carried no long-term grudges. He ran alongside his abuser like marathon runners on the same team.

One Saturday morning, as Theo painted the gutters on the front porch, he looked down from the ladder to see the daub of his father sitting on the smudge of swing near the front door. He could hear the knocking of ice cubes against a glass tumbler. Even from his beclouded perspective, Theo examined the strained hunch of his father's back against the swing. He could hear the struggle in his voice when he asked Theo, "Would you like some iced tea?"

"I'm good. Thanks, Dad," Theo answered.

Saturday afternoon for his father had always been Saturday *blowout*. His buddies opened and closed the Windjammer. "The only way to break a habit is to break it," his mother had told Theo. And Theo knew that his mom was by his father's side, inciting him to keep that habit broken. This was their second chance together.

"Master the dog, and you will master yourself." That is what Ahanu had told Theo. "The qualities that you deny and those you encourage are critical to mastering the dog," the Algonquin had said. "The kindness, loyalty, and strength that you shower upon the dog becomes who you are. Our souls are forged hard in such mastery because our mind and heart are concentrated on the worthy methods of training the dog."

Theo gravely watched his father as he earnestly wrestled with his soul. But Theo was no longer watching him through his eyes, which were so weak. He watched his father through his soul. Dreams are often the touchstones of our character. Despite his young age, Theo sensed his father's dreams. They were full of falling skies and quaking earth. He sensed his father battling with his habit as the cubes of ice continued to knock against the glass of his iced tea. *Breaking a routine can be murder*, Theo thought. While Theo knew prejudices were the real thieves of character, he also sensed that vices were life's true killers. Compelled by his rising empathy for his dad, Theo climbed down from his perch at the top of the ladder.

"Dad," Theo said as he walked onto the floor of the porch.

His prescription Ray-Bans across his eyes, his father remained in the wooden swing with his hands wrapped around the tumbler and his big legs stretched uncomfortably across the wood-planked floor of the porch.

Ted pulled out a gaudy yellow handkerchief with a riotous blue-and-red pattern. He wiped his brow with it. It tore against his forehead as if to break the plume of pride etched in his skin. Ted's hair had been cut short. Gone were the reckless locks of his handsome youth. He wore the mark of a penitent or a prisoner—a crown of nub. As Theo drew closer, the boy understood his father might break the glass with his thin, bare fingers.

"You know what Mrs. Shure, the librarian, told me?"

"What's that, Theo?" his father asked.

"God does not make junk."

Ted stared into his tumbler, the dwindling ice cubes sloshing at the bottom of the glass. His fidget finger tapped at the glass. Knocking the ice against the wall of the tumbler and turning his face upward, Ted looked at Theo.

"Therefore, I am not junk," said Theo.

"Yuh."

"And I came from you. You are not junk either, Dad. Just because you didn't shoot a gun in France or just because you didn't become an engineer, doesn't mean you are any less than any other man. Dad, both you and I have made mistakes, but we are not junk."

Ted leaned forward, placing his glass on the floor of the porch. He was quiet and then, finally, nodded.

"Yuh."

Slowly, Ted stood and pushed his green shades from his eyes to above his forehead. Looking directly at his boy, he walked toward him with purpose. Theo flinched, fearing his father was going to whack him.

"Forgive me, Theo," Ted said.

"I forgive you, Dad," Theo replied.

Then his father took him in his arms. Even though he was now thirteen, Theo allowed the embrace. It was strange to have the white, muscled arms of the assailant around his neck and shoulders. Theo clenched his mouth and made the best of it.

"I know I do not deserve you. I know I don't deserve your mom. I have asked her forgiveness too," Ted said softly.

In a few days, Theo got his new glasses in the mail. But something had happened to the boy when he had his limited sight. He found himself connected to the great world in which he lived.

"I have something for you, Dad. It is from one of my Boy Scout meetings," Theo said. His father had just finished his run. Ted and Shadow were both drinking water from the garden hose by the dinner bell.

Ted had recently told Theo that he had thought of helping out with the troop.

From the back pocket of his painting shorts, Theo pulled out a folded paper. Slowly, it opened to reveal mimeograph-blue words on a white page.

"What is it?" asked Ted.

"We have a number of guys from the tribe in my troop. So, as part of earning our Citizenship in Community merit badge, we need to learn each other's customs. The members from the tribe had to learn the Lord's Prayer. We had to memorize this prayer written by their chief over a hundred years ago."

Theo handed Ted the paper. "I thought you would like it."

"Thanks, son," Ted replied.

That night, while lying in bed next to Alice, Ted quietly read:

Give us hearts to understand;

Never to take from creation's beauty more than we give;

never to destroy wantonly for the furtherance of greed;

never to take from Nature what we cannot use.

Give us hearts to understand;

That to destroy earth's music is to create confusion;

that to ruin her appearance is to blind us to beauty.

Give us hearts to understand;

We have forgotten who we are.

We have sought only our own protection.

We have exploited simply for our own ends.

We have distorted our knowledge.

We have abused our power.

Great Spirit, whose dry lands thirst,

Help us to find the way to refresh your lands.

Great Spirit, whose waters are choked with debris, help us to find the way to cleanse your waters.

Great Spirit, whose beautiful earth grows ugly with misuse, help us to find the way to restore beauty to your handiwork.

Great Spirit, whose creatures are being destroyed, help us to find a way to replenish them.

Great Spirit, whose gifts to us are being lost in selfishness, help us to find the way to restore our humanity.

Oh, Great Spirit, whose voice I hear in the wind, whose breath gives life to the world, hear me; May I know your strength and wisdom. May I walk in your Beauty.

Ted read the poem several times, and then, he fell asleep.

Over the summer, Ted installed a new electrical system in the family pickup truck. In the evenings, Theo and Shadow would watch him work under a single industrial lamp hung in the barn. As an adult, Theo wanted to work on the inner workings of animals, and Ted seemed to be expert with the inner mysteries of machines. Theo observed that Ted's fingers, which always seemed to shake with nerves, had stilled as he gracefully handled the machine parts. There was not even a fidget from his fidget finger.

"How do you know all this stuff, Dad?"

"I dunno," Ted said with cheer in his voice. "It comes naturally."

"Why did you not finish with engineering?"

"I understood with my hands, Theo. But I could not always write it down or, sometimes, even read it. Yuh, can you see that? Not all the yelling in the world by Joseph Snow the Third could change that. Experts tested me. It seems my mind could not distinguish between left and right. So, for me, it was hard to read, let alone score well on tests. I understood but could not convey that understanding in ways acceptable to this society."

"I never knew Grandpa Snow," said Theo.

"Consider yourself fortunate, yes suh." In the deepest part of him, Theo knew in that instant that his grandfather had been a beater too.

One evening, the industrial light burned out just as Ted put Theo at the wheel to drive the truck out of the barn. The barn plummeted into darkness but for a moonbeam that broke through the roof. Ted looked up to see the roof damage from Hurricane Sally. As Shadow jumped into the bed of the truck, he watched the moonlight slanting through the roof as well.

"Yuh. I have to get that fixed," Ted said. "Winter will be here before we know it. We don't want any snow falling on our guests at the Christmas party." The hole remained. It did not get fixed. It would one day become a momentary salvation for Ted and the family before the ship they sailed on burned away.

Without grinding the gears, Theo pushed the stick shift into first gear, and the pickup truck slowly moved out of the barn and into the moon-drenched evening. In the lunar light, Theo realized his father was on the mend. A future was in sight.

Over the rest of the summer, Theo wrapped himself like a spinning top around that house again and again as he worked. When the sweetgum tree stopped dropping its gum-balls, Theo even painted that side of the house. In his many rotations, Theo's arms stretched wide with the white crisp paint of his brush and being, giving the house a new and glossy face.

As it was for the house, so it was for the family within.

CHAPTER TEN

Shadow walked past her yellow house. As Cleopatra lay in an early afternoon sunbeam at the end of her driveway, the white, long-haired cat appeared to examine Shadow with certain admiration. Not every animal had the courage or will to run. Some animals did not need to run, perfectly content in the human-clan into which they were born. Shadow, however, did run, and that was always impressive to fellow animals who had fallen under the spell of domestic comfort.

Running away from home life was simpatico to all animals, for each understood survival against the hurts. Humans could be cruel, violent, reckless, and destructive. Even though Cleopatra's sparkling blue eyes suggested respect, Shadow did not push his luck as he walked through the neighborhood that day. He did not attempt to kiss or play with her or even sniff her.

While Cleopatra never marked her territory, Shadow nevertheless knew into whose yard he was stepping. He knew not to walk the driveway unless she sanctioned the approach. She rose from her recline, leaving her position beneath the sunshine, and came over to him. He stopped at the end of the driveway, curious at her approach. Surprisingly, she rubbed her white fur softly against his golden side. Then she swatted him with her bushy tail—a sign to advance.

In that moment, he knew that a new *détente* had arrived.

In neighborly acknowledgment, he turned and sniffed her butt. She neither recoiled nor attacked. Shadow was delighted. He knew things between them were just going to get better.

It was Memorial Day. It had been almost three years since the war had ended. Theo would soon be fourteen. As Shadow led the way, the Snows walked into town for the parade. The white-clapboard town was dressed in the scalloped buntings of red, white, and blue.

Trumpets trumpeted. The high school band marched past the Soldiers' Memorial on the old town green. The town had erected the marble obelisk for the soldiers who fought in "the Rebellion" of 1861 to 1865.

Seeing his buddies in military uniform parade behind the county's beauty queen (carried in a cherry-red pickup truck) remained difficult for Ted. Afterward, Ted met the guys at the Windjammer, and while they drank, he sipped iced tea. Eventually, he joined the celebration with a few rum and cokes. At the barbecue that night at the house, Ted overcooked the meat.

When he apologized at the picnic table, he slurred his words.

"I'm sorry, sweetheart," Ted said, his eyelids heavy, his eyes half-closed. "It was just a few with the guys. Let it be. It's a holiday, after all!"

In the discovery, Alice's eyes went wide. Her proud, New England chin kept her head perfectly still.

"I swear, Ted Snow, you need to keep your word!"

In the evening, when Theo was really "trying to concentrate" on his homework and could not play fetch, Shadow would take his leave from the upstairs and walk down to the first floor.

In the dim downstairs, he searched for any light. Alice was industrious. She often worked late on a watercolor or oil painting in her studio.

In those sessions, Alice did not have much to say. So, Shadow would find Ted who would be in his study. In the winter months, there would be a fire in the small stone hearth, so Shadow could sit in the warmth and sparkle of the flames. Shadow was also permitted to sit in Ted's big comfy chair, so he could listen to what Ted had to say. He could not always understand the man, but he could always feel him.

Ted was not as animated in his tales as the boy was, but still, Ted was entertaining. In those times, they were called talks during "our little secret."

Once he locked the door to the study, Ted opened the bottom drawer of his desk. Shadow watched as Ted pulled a box of envelopes from the front of the drawer. Behind the box was an amber bottle of "our little secret."

Ted would stand the special bottle on the desk and gaze at it as if it were an ocean or a new baby or the most beautiful thing imaginable.

For Shadow, a waking dream would have been an extra-large and meaty bone from Flanagan's Meats. It would be wrapped in white butcher paper. With one snarl, Shadow would rip off the paper.

From the back of the top drawer, which held machines like scissors and staplers, Ted would pull out a small glass. Shadow never understood why a tall man like Ted would drink from such a short glass, but he supposed that was part of the secret too.

Shadow liked it best when Ted would smile at him, holding his glass with its little amber elixir, and "toast" him. Ted pressed the glass against Shadow's nose, proclaiming "to life." In response, Shadow huffed (rather than bark in front of Ted, who acutely disliked barking). Then Shadow would watch as Ted took the glass and drank the amber liquid in one gulp.

The first gulp was always the most interesting for Shadow to observe. Ted squeezed his eyes and his mouth into a puckered contortion as if the secret was tart by taste, like a bad tin of chicken from the dump. In the subsequent glasses, Ted's face contorted less and less as if he was growing accustomed to the taste. Ted sometimes pulled out his gaudy yellow handkerchief with the red-and-blue patterns and wiped his brow after he had his first drink from the tiny glass. It was as if he was somehow relieved.

Ted toasted Shadow often by saying, "Daddy Snow told me never to drink alone."

As Ted grew happier, he would lean back in his desk chair and tell stories to Shadow of when he was a boy and how he dreamed of being a big city engineer of great dams like Hoover or Boulder.

Eventually, Ted became sour in the juice of his disappointments, and his ruddy face grew as yellow as his handkerchief. He told the dog how he never fulfilled his potential and how he became "saddled" to the farm and the glassworks factory his father had bestowed to him. Shadow could not understand how Ted could have a saddle for he never saw him wearing one like Galileo and Cigar often wore.

Still, Shadow felt him. Shadow somehow knew the sunny horizon that broke every morning for him did not break in the same way for Ted. Ted might toast to "life," but somehow, Shadow did not feel that Ted was really part of life. Spring was in his heart, but winter ruled Ted's mind. Indeed, his one happiness seemed to be his own melancholy.

"Yuh, I like to drink. I like to forget life," Ted told the dog. He almost always told this to the dog before he fell asleep in the big chair. "Life is a horrible invention made by a stranger. It doesn't last. It's not good for anything. In the end, we all break our necks just trying to live!"

One night, Ted railed on top of his desk, the amber drink drained from the bottle. "I see him! I see him!" cried Ted, his voice thick, the puffy rings around his eyes blue with water and blood. "Can you see him, Shadow? He's in the corner! The Grim Reaper! But he's not getting me, you hear? You hear me? No, suh!"

His face cadaverous, Ted picked up the letter opener from the desk and jabbed it into the air, shouting at the reaper. He turned on the desk as if the dangerous thing was circling him. Ted kept turning and turning and turning. When Theo told stories, Shadow floated on them. When Ted told them, Shadow grew confused.

When Christmas came around and there was the first chill of winter, Shadow no longer had to search for the lights in the night. The light was all around him. There were electric candles in every window of the farmhouse. Shimmering white lights surrounded the large tin star on the side of the red barn. The tin star was legend. It could be seen all the way into town, floating above snowy Blueberry Hill in portentous splendor. Shadow would stand on the driveway, running in place as the tin star was hung, his white-linen paws battering against the icy gravel in excitement, thrilled.

Every year, a green balsam wreath with a bright red ribbon hung from the blueberry-blue door on the front porch.

Alice told Shadow a magical tale of the green wreath and the red ribbon. In the story, Father Sky, who reigned over the spirit, came to Mother Earth, who bore the form of a woman of clay named Mary. Sky and Earth married, and together they conceived a beautiful star child made of both spirit and earth.

The Star Child grew up and walked the world. The child of Father Sky and Mother Earth taught the world to live with the spirit in their clay hearts. Alice said the red of the holiday bow signified the Star Child's sacrifice, and the green balsam of the wreath signified the everlasting life that was for all people born to the spirit of Father Sky.

Shadow loved the story. It reminded him of his own sweet mother and the tales of Thunderbird who flew the skies in bird form in service to Gitche Manitou. Thunderbird was Shadow's guardian, just like Shadow was the guardian for Theo. Shadow adored the season of light. He always felt warm and cozy when it came around.

Of course, once the lights brought the season, the season brought the annual Christmas party. There was always snow from the sky by then. Shadow loved snow. *Time for rides on Theo's American Flyer Sled! Time for snowmen and snow-women! Time for snowballs in my face! Yippee!*

The Christmas party was held in the barn every year. It was a town pot luck, with the main meal provided by the Snow family. Since 1870, it had been an annual tradition. The Snow patriarchy, extending through the county, always gave of their abundance. They could afford to. They were the conquerors of the Algonquins.

The farmhouse was too small for such a large party. Alice, also, did not want salt from the snowy roads to be dragged through the old planked floors and ruin their oil finishes. Shadow, however, quite enjoyed licking the salt from the floor when snow boots occasionally made their way into the farmhouse.

The barn had an old oil tank; it was stout and stood on four steel legs. Some people said it looked like a cow. It was initially fuel to keep the winter animals—the horses, cows, and hens—from freezing. Now, the farm did not possess animals. There were just blueberries, vegetables, and tubers. Still, the oil tank in the barn heated the annual Christmas event, which always brought several hundred people to the top of Blueberry Hill.

For the annual party, large field tables were spread out on both floors of the barn for the food and drink. Oota Dabun and Ahanu Lightstone always came a week early. As they owned the largest Christmas tree farm in the area, they always donated two spruce trees for the party—one for the first floor of the barn and one for the second floor.

When on the hill, Oota Dabun always made it a point to seek Shadow out. "There's my kizis, my darling kizis," she would say, her string of delicate conch shells clacking about her neck. The dog kissed her more times than Oota Dabun Lightstone could ever count. She always came with an early Christmas present for the dog—a remnant of antler so thick Shadow was able to gnaw into its marrow until spring.

On the second floor of the barn, Santa Claus met with the children. There was also a small dance floor. The record player had been brought out from the living room of the house and installed on a table on the second floor of the barn. Extra speakers were fetched from the town hall, and the large barn was awash with the voices of Rosemary Clooney, Judy Garland, Frank Sinatra, Nat King Cole, and Bing Crosby singing everything from "Have Yourself a Merry Little Christmas" to "Little Drummer Boy."

On the first floor, a giant carousel contraption, a relic from an old Newport, Rhode Island mansion, anchored the center of the barn. The carousel was etched in Currier and Ives images of sleigh rides, carolers in mufflers, and skiers on a slope. The circle of red, green, and white glass spun around a massive arc light, casting dazzling figures of winter cheer across the faces and bodies of the happy partygoers. Big-boned boys danced with fine-boned girls. Not even Mr. Fezziwig, himself, could have dreamed of such a marvelous gadget as the Christmas carousel.

There was a table of ciders and sweets near Santa Claus's chair. Far from the kiddies' table, there was an adult table with spiked eggnog and fruitcakes steeped in rum. Alice ran the first floor because of the hot food, and Ted, in his red Christmas sweater, ran the second floor for the music, Santa Claus, and the food and drink snack tables. When people wanted drinks, they had to climb the stairs to brush against Santa on his throne.

Theo was on call to both Ted and Alice to run any last-minute errands—more garbage bags, more ice, or retrieving a random Christmas record from the house.

Everyone from town came—the baker, the librarians, the girls from the candy shop, the cashiers from Kresge's, the Reverend Cummings, and of course, the Lightstones. None of the Snows' immediate family came. Ted had successfully alienated them. His father had already passed. His mother, Cailleach Snow, never travelled at night. Her chauffeur charged her overtime for evening hours. Still, there was laughter, dancing, and general goodwill from the hundreds who attended.

When Theo was asked by Ted to get the *Dean Martin Christmas Album* from the house, he could smell the scent of rum on his father's breath. Furrowing his brow, Theo looked at his father carefully. The yellow skin on Ted's face had returned. Theo had been told that when you had the disease his father had, any drinking could lead to an unhappy ending.

"Are you alright, Dad?" Theo asked softly. Of course, Ted knew what he was really asking.

"Yup, Theo. I had to make sure the eggnog was strong enough."

"Dad," Theo said with disappointment.

"Theo, 'tis the season. I have it under control. I promise. Run along now." But Ted could not back up his promise, for sadly, unknown to Theo, Ted was already drunk. But, as there was so much joy and cheer at the event, no one, not even Theo, fully understood its gravity.

"Dad, I'll stay here and help you," Theo replied, straightening up the cups and napkins on the adult table.

"I need two more bags of ice and the *Dean Martin Album*. Okey?" said Ted with a sternness in his voice.

"Okey dokey," Theo responded, casting a wary look at his father.

As Theo hurried down the pine stairway to the first floor, Ted had the time to retreat to the dark corner of the barn. Shadow walked with Ted. Shadow knew the drill. He would stay with Ted for Ted had promised Daddy Snow that he would never drink alone.

There in the dark, beneath a tackle box and against a pocked wall, Ted had hidden his own bottle of Captain Morgan Rum. Shadow watched as Ted tilted the Captain upside down and guzzled from the head of the pirate. Not understanding why there was no glass or no toasting, Shadow barked to interrupt Ted, to remind him that he needed to say his words.

"What's ta' matter, Shadow, can't keep a secret?" Laughing, Ted turned the bottle on the dog and, with a jerk, splashed him with the remains of the rum from Captain Morgan's head. Instantly, Shadow shook himself, attempting to rid the sticky-sweet liquor from his fur. Ted's face quickly grew dark, unknowable to Shadow. Sensing his danger, Shadow barked as if Ted were a stranger. The music and chatter from the crowd was too loud and chaotic to hear any barking. When Ted raised his hand, leveling a "get out" command at the dog, Shadow obeyed. He left the corner and climbed down the wooden steps to the party on the first floor.

With so much weight on the electrical power, it was standard tradition at the Snow Christmas party for a surge to blow a fuse. While the carousel lamp was a welcome addition to the festivities, it was an antique with old cords that heavily taxed the electrical system. The crowd shouted and swayed throughout the barn as, like a strobe, the lights pitched on and off until the barn went dark. Ted made his way to the fuse box for the third time that evening. When the lights came back on, the crowd *hurrahed*.

The dancing resumed, bone to bone, soul to soul. But the excitement of the dance did not stir Ted. He leaned against the corner beam. He slid down to the floor in a drunken sleep. When Theo returned with the two bags of ice for the adult table, he could not find his father. Theo simply emptied the bags into the almost-empty ice chests as Nat King Cole crooned:

> Joy to the world!
> The Lord is come;
> Let earth receive her King.

At ten o'clock that night, the arc lamp inside the carousel exploded like a Christmas cracker. The old machine threw sparks everywhere. The glints fell like fiery rain on the merry proceedings, igniting the crepe-paper streamers and the pine garlands. The heat from the furnace had made the beams and floorboards extremely dry.

It was not long before there were pockets of flame throughout the two stories of the barn. Meanwhile, the music of Nat King Cole continued to play from the portable record player on the second floor:

> Let every heart prepare Him room,
> And heaven and nature sing,
> And heaven and nature sing,
> And heaven, and heaven, and nature sing!

CHAPTER ELEVEN

The party goers stamped their snow boots at the flames, but the fire spread too rapidly. As Alice shouted above the music, the crowd hurried out of the barn. Theo ran to grab the fire extinguishers from the shed, but since the double doors to the barn opened onto Blueberry Hill so the guests could escape, the wintry air blew its cold oxygen on the flames. It was a bellows encouraging hearth embers. *Whoosh.* The flames on the first floor whipped the conflagration all the way to the rooftops.

The baker, Lynette Magruder, scrambled into the house and called the fire department. Alice shouted into the cavernous space, making certain everyone had left.

Even through the smoke and ash in the yard, Theo could smell the rum on his dog's fur. He looked through the crowd and could not see his father. He leaned down and whispered to Shadow, "Where is Dad, Shadow? Where is Dad?" As soon as he heard Theo say dad, Shadow dashed inside the barn and started up the burning steps.

"No, Shadow!" Theo shouted as he chased his dog.

"Theo!" Alice cried. "You have to leave the barn, Theo!" She grabbed onto her son's blazer as he ran past her.

"It's Dad." Theo screamed. "He must still be up there!"

Alice's face blanched.

When Theo turned around to look for Shadow, the dog was already halfway up the burning stairway, his fur as wild and golden as the flames through which he darted, his tiger-striped chest engorged, armored for struggle.

As Shadow reached the second floor, the stairway broke behind him. Part of the upper floor fell away. Barrels and tables and the Lightstone Christmas tree dropped to the floor of the barn like toys.

As the vinyl of the Christmas album melted under the heat, the music of Nat King Cole spilled into wax on the needle. Nat's voice slowed and then stopped in the middle of his chestnuts-roasting-on-an-open-fire crooning.

The screeching sound of approaching fire engines filled the thin air. Images of sleigh rides and carolers poured away from the carousel lantern, leaving only a bright flame where the carousel bulb once burned.

The fire on the second floor of the barn moved like a wave from the epicenter of the stairwell. An old tractor plow blade fell from its storage bracings like a knife slicing an onion, falling across the haunches of the dog, driving him to the burning floor. Shadow yelped from the excruciating pain. Even in the heat, he smelled his own blood.

Fighting against the agony, the dog yanked his body from the plow blade, setting his dark eyes on the fuse box. But something had happened to his legs. Driven by the flow from his adrenals, Shadow sailed with as much speed as he could muster across the waves of heat to the corner of Dad's little secret. The flames bit at his paws as he struggle-ran to the corner of the barn. The fuse box was now in flames, emitting smoke so dense and black, it had to be toxic.

There was nothing heroic about the scene into which Shadow arrived. Ted was not trapped by fallen debris. He was bound, immoveable, by the rum-induced sleep of his jag. The oppressive smoke hung like a wall across his face. When he awoke to Shadow's forceful pull on his sweater, Ted looked in shock at the smoke. Shadow grabbed the belt at Ted's waist and began pulling him to the center of the barn. But it was no use. The floor was in flames. The stairway had disappeared.

Shadow looked above at the fuming roof. There was a hole at the low side of the roofing. Shadow had observed it during the summer Ted and Theo worked on the truck engine. It was the damage left by Hurricane Sally. The dog dropped the man and leapt at the roof from the floor.

He jumped again and again until he forced open a wider portal in the vulnerable, patched tar. He dragged the man by the belt and brought Ted to the portal. He barked loudly at the man. Ted groggily awoke. Shadow poked and prodded him as Ted grabbed at the hole in the roof. Ted yanked himself onto the rooftop. Then he turned and pulled Shadow up. Shadow's back side was covered in blood. Ted's nostrils were silver as if he had inhaled bullets.

From the rooftop, Shadow looked down, barking at the firefighters. To raise his voice against the noise below, Shadow dug his charred paws into the tar of the roof and wailed.

It was a howl from the snow-filled heavens so powerful it cut like a razor into the jangled chaos below.

"On the roof!" cried Ahanu Lightstone in his timbered, rich voice. Fingers and arms jutted upward to the rooftop, pointing to the dog. Ahanu helped a firefighter with the steel ladder. The fire chief shouted into the megaphone. Additional ladders skittered up the siding of the red barn but, remarkably, even with the extensions, they were too short for the high roof of the barn.

Shadow watched as a circle of men and women held wide a round safety net of canvas. The people were as small as the passengers on Theo's Lionel Train set.

"Jump, jump," they cried.

Shadow discerned the voice of the first man who ever called to him. It was Ahanu. He had joined the firefighters and many in the community. He was holding the circled net with the other people. In his pain and panic, Shadow glimpsed the circle of stone that Ahanu and Oota Dabun had once danced around, praying for strength and protection for Shadow and the Lost Boys.

"Jump. Jump."

Shadow understood what jump meant, but what about in this circumstance? As the fire moved like a wave across the tarred roof, the dog assumed the white net below might, indeed, save Ted's life. Since he trusted Ahanu, Shadow knew there could be no harm. He barked to the people below and then dragged the man by his belt to the gutter of the barn.

When the people below saw the prostrate body of Ted rolling toward the gutter, they screamed in relief and worry.

Every rhythm prepares a future. The prayers sung, the drums that beat around the stone circle of the fire pit so long ago, still rang. In the icy air, Shadow felt the tremendous rhythm of Thunderbird's wings beating at his own ribs.

Shadow became those wings as he rolled Ted's body over the rooftop and into the charcoal-colored air. He watched as Ted shrunk before his eyes, disappearing into the folds of the life net.

"Jump, Shadow! Be a good boy! Jump!" cried the voice over the megaphone. It was the voice of his master.

The dog looked down again at the small jar-cap of the safety net. There was no other way. He leapt. His fall was so fast, the dog had no time to think. He dropped into the net held by Ahanu and the people. Immediately, the firemen ran with the net, away from the barn. Traveling inside the gauze, Shadow sensed they had run a mile, but the firefighters were only getting clear of the barn.

Vroommm!

A swell of energy rose. Shadow's ears shot straight up at the shock of the rupture. The oil tank inside the barn exploded, splattering almost sixty gallons of oil onto the already fiery night. The cars near the barn flew into the air. The guests screamed, running farther from the expanding inferno.

A fireball ascended into the night, pushing the roof and its debris into the snowy ether. Shouting through a megaphone, the fire chief urged the crowd to stay back.

Shadow poked his head out of the canvas fold. Delirious, he was as hot and wild as the fireball lifting in the night. Debris rained across the onlookers in shards of smoking wood, bits of tar, and bright embers. Women and men shooed the downward catastrophe from their hair with their hats and gloves.

The five-pointed tin star gracing the side of the barn fell. Shadow looked about. He saw Alice stooped by the stretcher that held Ted, his eyes closed. There was a mask over his face and oxygen tanks by his side. The ambulance light turned as Alice kissed Ted on the forehead.

His hair dusted in snowflakes, Theo cried out as he came toward Shadow. "Hold still, boy. Hold still." Theo grew closer. "Dr. Cook is going to give you a shot to ease your pain. It's only a sting. It's only a little sting, boy!"

As Theo reached him, he dropped to the ground, weeping. Dr. Cook, in his reindeer sweater, wiping the snow from his thick, round eyeglasses, approached the canvas net.

Shadow could not understand why Theo was crying and carrying on so. Thunderbird had kept true to the stirrings of the drums. He came to the aid of both Shadow and Ted. *Everyone is safe*, he thought.

Oota Dabun came toward him. Her bright violet eyes were filled with tears. She whispered a prayer in her native tongue.

As the firefighters opened the safety net, Shadow observed the canvas streaked with bright-red blood. It took him a moment to realize what had happened. Dr. Cook plunged the needle into his shoulder. The blood was his. In morphine and adrenalin, he floated. Before he swam away, he noticed that his right back leg was missing. He remembered. It had been torn off by the falling plow blade. He could feel his severed leg on the second floor of the barn. It grew hot, burning in the flames.

CHAPTER TWELVE

At the hospital, Theo studied his father's hands. In earlier days, those hands had been dangerous. Now, as Hercules faded from consciousness, those hands were oblivious to harm, almost tender in their dying. As the tension drained from his father's fidget finger and went limp, Theo wondered. *What is it to die?* It was a slipping away from the world and so to die was nothing. But not to have lived, that was terrible. Theo's sorrows were deep for his father. He thought his father's disenchantments kept him from much of the experiences of life. Theo observed that his father's hair had grown long again, unruly and gray. Now, it lay matted against his skull, dense from smoke and fever.

In the hospital room, Ted Snow apologized to Theo and Alice for his weakness. His voice was raspy. Dry. Frail. His lungs were nothing more than parched tissue paper. In fevered delirium, he sat up as if seeing a ghost, shouting, "Daddy? Is that you, Daddy?" His eyes were stripped of starlight. His look held shocked oblivion. Whether reaper or angel, the vision fleeted. He fell back on the pillow. At around three that morning, he gained consciousness. He spoke his contritions. He had wanted to do better, but "somehow," he told them, "I did not have the strength, not within me, nor by God."

Theo winced.

It was a sad state of affairs when your father blamed the master of the universe for his own weaknesses. For Ted, his struggles were apparently too big even for eternity. "Master the dog and in so doing, you shall master yourself," Ahanu Lightstone had told Theo. His father had never become his own master. As his ghost continued to slip from his body, his father once again grew fevered. His final words were delivered in a scream. "No, suh! No, suh!"

"Too small, too weak to get his demons behind him," Theo later wrote in his journal, full of the hard, tragic judgment children have when their parents disappoint them so severely. Theo believed that men did not escape from life because life was too small, but life escaped from men when men were too small.

Meanwhile, at a clinic in town, miles from the hospital, Shadow underwent surgery on his back right haunch below his tail. The plow blade had severed the leg below the rump. Earlier, Dr. Cook had staunched the bleeding with a firmly wrapped tourniquet. Now, Cook sewed his skin together. Heavily sedated, Shadow fell asleep on the silver table. The veterinarian phoned Alice at the hospital and told her that Shadow had lost blood but would survive.

Later, Dr. Cook slept in a cot next to the dog he had once called "the runt." Still dressed in his reindeer sweater, he stayed with Shadow until morning.

Walt Whitman wrote, "After you have exhausted what there is in business, politics, conviviality, and so on, one finds that none of these finally satisfy, or permanently wear—what remains? Nature remains."

On December 12, 1948, just after the first snowfall of the season, Nature claimed her own. Ted Snow succumbed to the fate of his burned and flimsy lungs. He never got the chance to help out with Theo's Boy Scout troop. He never took the opportunity to fully give up his prejudices. Hercules died of asphyxiation. Ted Snow was thirty-two years old.

Theo drove the station wagon back from the hospital. He and his mother rode in silence. They had been at the hospital all night. A light snow fell into the dawning light. As they approached Blueberry Hill, the snowfall had mercifully covered the blackened debris that had once held a barn. Nuthatches and chimney swifts darted in the winter mist. There was virtually nothing left but the tin star, now propped against the gray bark of the sweetgum tree.

The four legs and metal basin of what was left of the oil tank stood in the midst of the snowy field like a decapitated cow. Like a tightrope walker, a black phoebe balanced its body against the edge of the shattered tank.

Alice shuddered as the car passed the smoldering barn. Theo watched from the side of his eyes as she gnawed on her fist to keep back her tears.

"Thank God. The house wasn't touched," she said softly.

Theo said nothing. He understood that his mother was wound as tight as the alarm clock he had once stowed in Shadow's crate. As close as he was with his mom, there were certain things left unsaid—principally, Alice's relationship with her husband. In front of Theo, she had never said an unkind thing about Ted. She never said anything stronger than "she was worried for him," or "every man or woman must face their demons alone. We can only be there for them. We must be there for your dad."

When they walked into the kitchen, Alice did not switch on the overhead light. There was enough illumination from the broadening sunrise. Theo observed his mother's walk to the coffee percolator. Her walk was weighted. In the grief, her shiny party shoes had grown heavy. Gone was the young woman who could change the atmosphere with her kindness or her smile. She scooped coffee from the Chock Full o'Nuts can into the filter at the top of the percolator. A golden sunbeam slanting through the window of the sink caught her abundant auburn hair, imparting both a warmth and a gloss.

She turned the pot on. Theo observed how pale her face had become. The room went silent. She stood guard at the counter. Like a dream, Theo heard the *tick-tick-tick* of the small jeweled watch around her wrist. Her eyes grew as big as blowlamps. She turned like a ghost, floating. She wafted out of the kitchen and down the hallway while Theo scrambled after her. She moved into Ted's study and threw open the doors to the desk. She opened cabinet after cabinet until she found the bottle of Captain Morgan at the back of the bottom drawer. She pulled it up to the light at the window and saw that only an inch remained of the yellow-gold liquid. She dropped the bottle to the floor, and it landed with a crash.

She walked to the cupboard by the hearth. It was the same shape of cupboard that Theo had used to make a bed for Shadow. She opened the door and pulled out the wood at the front of it. Behind it, she found a stack of full bottles. She pulled the bottles out—scotch, chartreuse, bourbon, and rum.

Like a force of Nature, and indeed Alice was, she threw the bottles into the cavernous empty hearth. Not even her love or the power of the Snow patriarchy or the wealth of the Old Colony Railroad could save Ted from Ted.

Not knowing what to do or say because he had never seen his mother so vulnerable, Theo ran to her and pulled her hands to his awkward teenage body, fearful that she might injure herself with the exploding glass.

"He tried, Mom. Dad tried!" he cried in confusion as he

gathered her arms into his.

In anger, she pulled away to throw more of the bottles into the fireplace. But he grabbed her and brought her with him to the floor. She fought his arms, but they were strong.

"He tried?" she screamed. "It is not enough to try!" she screamed again. "He promised *me*! He promised *us*!" Theo and Alice were left alone in the lonely room in an empty house without dog or man.

The archaeology of grief is not ordered. It is earth under a spade. Grief turns up belongings long forgotten. Surprising things come to light. Not only memory. States of mind. Emotions. Old ways of seeing. But Alice would not live in remorse or despair. For so many years, Alice altered her life by altering her attitude. The blows that Ted lay on her did not change. *She* changed. This was a time when wives often lived with the damages of their husbands to protect their children. She grew a tougher shell. She became numb to him and, in so doing, allowed Ted to do with her what he would.

That winter was a long one, yet Alice would not allow the ever-present grief to turn her soul into a land of remorse. Still the rhythms that metered from the tragedy of the Christmas party continued to ripple in the long, long days. It is impossible to stop cadence. A bell rings long after the clapper hits the cup.

It was a time without fathers. It was a time without dogs. But Alice, who had trained herself to be a spark that could ignite a room, would not allow the farmhouse to become a coffin for her and her son. Instead, that winter, by her attitude, it became a cocoon. Against the chilling brume, Alice and Theo held each other in their strength and sorrow, knowing, somehow, somewhere, a butterfly might soar again from the casing of silk hanging in the winter wind.

After the accident, Theo walked every day to the animal clinic. There were always the same tracks in the snow: people, snowshoes, the pads of rabbits, the pads of four-legged dogs. Even such tracks made Theo sad, but he found the way to beat back the grief. He needed to be constant for the dog.

Shadow recovered slowly. The shock did not leave him. There was internal bleeding. He developed an infection. Yet, Shadow never whined or whimpered, and he was always happy to see his boy.

Eventually, Shadow would walk again; the doctor was sure of it. The loss of his leg and Ted had driven the great wolf to depression. It was a great emptiness.

Theo remained strong for his boy and never got choked up in front of him. But every night, Theo returned home exhausted from his visits at the clinic.

"It's not fair," Theo said in the kitchen.

"When Shadow saved your father, he did not do what was fair, Theo. Shadow did what was right."

At the doctor's clinic on Main Street, Theo was impressed with both the power and acumen of Dr. Cook's attentive touch. Theo truly saw the doctor in his work. He observed both confidence and patience in the way the man treated Shadow. Over time, Alice encouraged the relationship between Dr. Cook and Theo, for she saw the doctor as a role model.

"Walk with me. Walk with me, buddy!" Theo incanted as he coached Shadow pied-piper style across the grass in the front yard of the farmhouse. "What a good boy!" Shadow grew accustomed to his tripod status. Eventually, Theo inspired

Shadow to walk up the stairs and down the stairs.

Shadow figured if Mighty Dog could carry houses with his bare paws, he could surely manage Blueberry Hill with only three legs. Besides, Shadow knew the Tree of Life as Thunderbird perched in her branches. He was Nature with a "capital N" as Ralph Waldo Emerson, the naturalist of Massachusetts, had so often stated. "Nature is always capitalized because Nature is a treasure from the Divine," Emerson wrote.

Shadow was given a second chance to walk the world. It was not long before he could scale not only the hill, but he could make his way through the high bramble.

Theo tried his best to let his bitterness over Ted go. It seemed easier for Shadow. One late winter's day, Theo cleaned Shadow's cubby and found Ted's yellow handkerchief at the back of it. The one with the gaudy dabs of blue and red. It was chewed and dirty. Theo threw it in the trash basket next to his desk. Shadow fished it out.

"Whaddaya want with that slobbery old piece of cloth?" Theo asked.

Shadow looked at Theo with his big, dark eyes. The dog walked to the cubby, putting the yellow handkerchief back where it belonged, so that when he lay sleeping, the cloth could be close to his heart.

"You're a better man than I," Theo said.

CHAPTER THIRTEEN

Once the spring crocuses had pushed through the loamy soil, Theo took Shadow to Cockle Cove Beach to, once more, find their North Star. Everywhere, the early flowers were up; their petals bent toward the sun, awash in the dreaming directive to follow the sunshine. Beneath the canopy of Red, the cedar tree, Shadow lay in the mulch. The cedar waxwings cried their thin, lisping song in the nearby fruit trees. Shadow hobbled on three legs from the bluff to the sand. As he swam in the Atlantic, he gave himself over to Nature. In the chill spring water, the mother's warm fingers touched his paddling shoulders and haunches. As he swam, his body rebalanced to the soothing cadence of her murmurs.

Theo witnessed the power of the sea on Shadow's equilibrium. Shadow began to discover harmony with only three legs. Convinced Nature's power was the best medicine for his dog, Theo returned almost every day after school so that Shadow could swim the blue ocean.

When he plunged into the sea, Shadow held the voltage of her tides in his haunches. The electrical power of the waves sparked through his golden ears, jilting them upright. His paws rode the slippery seaweed. His red tongue lollygagging and his dark eyes wide, he immersed himself in the water as if he were the brine itself. He tasted the vigor of the ever-swelling world on his tongue.

Day by day, Shadow's walking improved. One afternoon after his swim, Shadow climbed the bluff to Red. When he reached Theo, he began to sprint around him in a circle, herding him like he had done as a puppy. The river of life flows around barriers. It finds new ways to reach its destination. The missing leg no longer defined him. The disability had grown into strength. Theo watched as Shadow fell asleep on his back like an upturned table, his three legs comfortably jutting into the air. It was then that Theo knew Shadow would be just fine.

After that spring by the sea, Shadow decided he would return to the neighborhood.

The brown boxer, Zeus, was cantankerous as ever and barked as soon as he saw Shadow rounding Cockle Cove Road. It did not matter at all to the brown barking dog whether Shadow had two legs or three legs or four legs. He simply barked. Shadow could only sigh. *The old adage from the humans is true*, thought Shadow. *You can't teach old dogs new tricks. Zeus was sour before, and Zeus is sour now!*

The chagrin Shadow felt about Zeus being incapable of change weighed heavily on him. Zeus was not unlike Ted Snow, who could not travel to further lands. In the end, the only place Ted would go was the Windjammer. The sorrow Shadow felt for Zeus surprised even him, for Shadow did not really like the boxer. Shadow knew Zeus was missing so much of the world. Zeus did not travel down Cockle Cove Road or Ulysses Road or to the county dump where the fragrances of sweet, mean life were profound. He never dreamed of Mount Olympus. He never even climbed to Blueberry Hill. Zeus simply stayed in his corner lot and howled. Shadow felt bad for Zeus. It was that universal sorrow all dogs, who think deeper and live richer, feel toward their fellow dogs who simply want to know comfort and stay clear of the vast adventures of which Shadow's mom spoke.

It was completely different with Cleopatra.

The yellow house, the Turnblacer's house, was several houses down from Zeus's. When Shadow rounded the road, he saw Cleopatra at the end of the driveway. Before her was her silver supper bowl. She had dragged the bowl all the way from the house to the end of the drive. It held a mound of wet, pink mash. Having been raised on dry kibble and occasional gravy from the fry pan, Shadow did not know this fragrance wafting up from the silver supper bowl.

Cleopatra meowed and told Shadow that it was *fish*. Her people called it *tuna*. She called it *supper*.

"I want you to have it," she said in animal-cant.

"But why?" he replied in his venerable tongue.

"You did not bury yourself in the ocean when you thought of drowning that night in the storm."

"How did you know that?"

"I am a cat. We know the wind."

"But that was so long ago . . ."

Cleopatra seemed to be looking at Shadow with new and open eyes. Like all cats, she bore a special mysticism, but this cat was especially exotic. Henry David Thoreau once said, "What sort of philosophers are we, who know absolutely nothing of the origin and destiny of cats?"

"But most importantly," Cleopatra continued, "you saved your master's father from the fire."

"That was my destiny."

"No," she said. "We have a choice. You saved the father of your master. You saved yourself from drowning. So please, eat of my supper. You are my Bastet."

Shadow was confused. "Who is Bastet?"

"Bastet is the ruler of the ancient cat, the mau. Bastet brought wisdom to mau."

"I am a dog, Cleopatra."

"You have seen the world, so you are wise. You have been to the five and dime. You have entered the temple of books. The gulls tell me you are the ruler of the sea, even with but three legs. Eat, for you need your nourishment, my noble traveler."

"I do not know what to say," Shadow said. *How did she drag the silver bowl to the end of the driveway? How does she manage to speak so intelligently?* Shadow was convinced that her master had also read *Animal Farm* to her.

"Do not say," she answered. "Eat."

Shadow came before her.

He leaned into the silver bowl and nuzzled it. It smelled wonderful. He looked up at the long-haired cat.

At one time, she had hissed at him, arched her back against him. Now, she encouraged him to eat from her very own supper bowl. He could smell her breath on the bowl and on the mound. With her electric-blue eyes, she watched him. He looked away from her and ate. It was the first time Shadow had every dined on tuna fish.

The stink of the meal was even more profound than the thousand smells of the dump. As he luxuriated in the tuna, he thought of Bastet and Thunderbird and the Star Child and even Napoleon, the boar from *Animal Farm*. The older he grew the more Shadow became certain that it made no difference what words the dogs or cats or humans of this earth used to tell the same story. The profound truths reside beyond the purview of one language, one continent, one species. The divine is available to all life when spirit-eyes are used to observe the reality that breathes beyond the senses.

Outside of the turkey sandwich and Thanksgiving chestnut stuffing, the tuna in the cold silver bowl was the most delicious meal Shadow had ever had. It was not only the exotic tuna, but it was also Cleopatra's breath that made the meal delicious.

Shadow had once been her enemy, but Cleopatra never again hissed at the dog. Cleopatra found him majestic. He was her blemished monarch. When he walked down from Blueberry Hill, she watched the blue air shimmer off his golden tail. The gulls spoke of his rule over the ocean. Now, she witnessed that reign in his powerful essence.

Before her empty silver bowl, Cleopatra proclaimed Shadow the King of Sea and Sky. "All of Nature knows," she said.

In August of that year, the sky was incandescent with the Perseid meteor showers. Shadow and Theo found a beach free of sky watchers. Together, boy and dog howled at the black sky as the white streaks of burning meteor rained in the night. Shadow was startled by the deep resonance of Theo's voice. With the death of Ted, Shadow witnessed many tears from Alice. But he had never seen his master cry. Now, he howled as a magnificent star crumbled from the heavens and fell to earth.

Theo had changed too. With Theo getting older, the fantasy of boyhood gave way to an ardent curiosity of Nature. Summer turned to autumn. The apple orchards rose in crimson crowns. The flickering corn jutted toward the sun. The red-winged blackbirds and the yellow-rumped warblers flew through orange skies. In Alice's garden, the heirloom tomatoes withered. Now, in the wake of the tomatoes, acorn squash, butternut squash, and pumpkins waxed plump in the abundant soil beds.

As the days grew shorter, like magic, the maple and elm trees were ablaze in a colorful opera. The crisp, cool air grew redolent with the odor of sap. Conifers lay like secret treasures in nests of browning needles. Orange, red, and plum-hued leaves shivered in the erected air. Soon, the brown thrashers were barely discernible in the folding, dying leaves of the elms.

With Ted gone, Shadow made certain he walked every room every morning in the house on Blueberry Hill. He became the sentient one, instilling the house with his own prevailing presence. In time, the dog filled the empty rooms with something new. It was his own creatureliness. He brought the fragrance of cultivated nature into the rooms of the farmhouse. It was his own scent, not unpleasant, a mix of the smells from Alice's garden, crushed acorns, peat, ripening apples, and sea salt. This was *cultivated* Nature, not the wood but the living garden, where god and man met, where wolves became dogs and potatoes grew to feed the world. As he toured the rooms, Shadow brought the sweet, mean taste of life onto the freshly ironed cotton and the polished maple floors. That was the alchemic Nature of any dog when he or she was loved by a household. By that dog, the house became a home.

For a while, the screeching of the kitchen door ceased. Theo oiled the hinges. What once was familiar and grating was now new again with just the simplest of care.

A small November sun hung in the sky. The family enjoyed the peace that came from attentive solicitude. And that Thanksgiving, the first Thanksgiving without Ted (who had often come to the feast table in his sunglasses), Alice, Theo, and Shadow were not alone. The Lightstones came with food and drink and merry vitality.

"They are *not* filthy injuns," said Alice to Theo. "On this, your dad got it wrong. They are us, Theo. The Snows pushed the Algonquins from their own land. They did this by demonizing them, not seeing them as human. To take their land we called them 'demons,' 'savages.' It is easy to kill a demon. It is much harder to kill a man. But, in the deepest way, we are together with them. They, too, were given a sacred gift. They, too, were given life." Alice set her mouth as she looked at her son.

"I know, Mom," Theo said, softly. "I got my merit badge in World Community."

Shadow did not realize that this Thanksgiving was made especially for him. He had been sad about not being able to keep Ted alive. But at the Thanksgiving dinner that year, after all the aloneness, there was a party. Ahanu and Oota Dabun Lightstone, Shadow's first human parents, made the dinner into a party.

Oota Dabun whispered in his ear. She told him that his first mother, Wendy, now flew with Thunderbird. Apparently, she crossed the bridge in the spring when he was still mending. Nothing had really changed since her crossing. Despite the distance in land or in time, Wendy was always with him. Always. Just as he was forever with his many brothers. In his dreams, they played.

The Lightstones brought a fully roasted twenty-pound turkey, acorn and butternut squash from the Lightstone garden, green beans, and rhubarb pie. Ahanu wore a sparkling, red-beaded shirt. Oota Dabun wore a bright violet dress that matched her eyes. Around her neck, by a braided silver chain, hung a hammered silver circle engraved with the Tree of Life, blooming with countless flowers.

With Ahanu guiding him, Theo carved the turkey at the kitchen table. Theo's hands were steady. For years, he had watched Ted's hands slice the bird. The meat was cut thick and jagged. Now as the man of the house, Theo's grasp was precise, even strategic.

"I wish to give thanks tonight to Shadow. Had it not been for Shadow, we would never have met," Ahanu said, his hands folded in prayer. "In honor of Shadow and in honor of your god, I should like to say your Lord's Prayer at the feast table in my native language," he said softly as if he were already in deep thought. "If you would be at peace with that?"

"We are," answered Theo.

"Of course we are," answered Alice.

Ahanu bowed his head and took the hand of his wife and the hand of Alice. Theo completed the circle of belonging by taking the other hand of Oota Dabun and Alice. Shadow watched from his seat on the floor.

Quitianatammnach koowesunonk, Peyaunmoonteh kukke-tassootamóonk, Kuttenauntamóunk ne n nach ohkeït neäne kesukqut

Shadow's golden tale wagged. He was delighted with the song of the heavens that came tumbling from Ahanu's mouth.

Gada. Gada. Gada.

As was his want, Shadow stayed beneath the table. He nudged the trousers and skirts of those in attendance.

Oh, I love Thanksgiving!

At his prompting, every hand reached down with turkey and bread and, every once in a while, his favorite delicacy, a chestnut plucked from the stuffing.

Later, Shadow watched Ahanu and Theo say goodbye on the porch. Their hot breath streamed like banners against the cold night.

"How are you, really, since the death of your father?" asked Ahanu.

"I am numb," Theo replied. He looked out at the sweetgum tree. Its scorched gold leaves turned in the wind of the indigo-black night.

Ahanu lay his hand on Theo. "Don't be afraid to weep, Theo. Those who do not cry can never really see."

Then it happened. Shadow saw it, too, after all the many months. Theo wept in front of the strapping Algonquin. As Theo's shoulders shook, Ahanu, a grandfather many times over, embraced the youth.

"Yes, cry. Cry it out, my son. Let it go. Do not let his ghost own you."

"I am sorry," Theo said.

"There, there."

"I never cry."

"There, there. It's fine. It's fine."

Ahanu patted the boy's shoulder.

Shadow watched as a magic mist seemed to engulf their embrace. It was like the mist that rose from Ahanu and Oota Dabun's fingers, growing into a specter all the many years ago. The specter was Alice holding a reddened child. Now between Ahanu and Theo, it was a mist of beginning.

"Let it out, my son. Then never look back, unless going

backwards is your destination. Light swallows darkness. Compassion eats fear. You are to bring the word of the animosh to the people. For life is romance as well as science. Onward, Theo. Onward. There, there. There, there."

Theo continued weeping, and with each tear, he marched his way into manhood.

Every rhythm prepares a future.

"There, there."

CHAPTER FOURTEEN

With Ted gone, it seemed that the heavy days were over. There were no longer the exchanged and panicked glances between Theo and Shadow. *The storm was on the move.* There wasn't much that needed to be spoken in words between Shadow and Theo. How ya doin', thataboy, walk with me, don't worry, and I'll be back were usually enough.

But, sometimes, Shadow worried about those places Theo had to attend on his own—school, the temple, or the car for driver's education, even though Theo was a pretty good driver already.

Sometimes, when Theo would return to Shadow after a day at the land known as "school," Theo's face was gray and his body energy-less.

"That's life," Theo said to his dog as he shrugged his ever-expanding shoulders, leaned down, and petted Shadow. "There's just a lot of information to learn, boy—and charts and diagramming sentences and pi."

When he heard that final word, happily, Shadow jumped on Theo's knee. "Not that kind of pie, not blueberry, or rhubarb, but mathematical pi," said Theo with a sigh.

On those days of the gray mask, Shadow knew it would take Theo a long time to return to laughter, to the place where he would want to throw the ball or run through the salt marshes, chasing the milky-white egrets. Where there might be blueberries and strawberries, *somewhere*. That was part of Shadow's job description: to return his master to the joy found in Nature—to the green grass, the sandy bluffs, the foamy laciness of the tides.

On the gray days when Theo returned with the gray mask, Shadow, from the floor of the bedroom, raised his head and simply stared, his eyes locking on Theo's eyes.

Like a child in a stare-down contest, Shadow did not break the glance. "Come on!" Theo was uncertain of whether the dog wanted to relieve himself or was simply studying him. Since the funny papers smack so many years ago, Shadow never barked.

He *stared* for the necessary attention. Sometimes, he let out a shrill whine from the well of his throat, like the buzzing of a bee. Now, he only glared at Theo.

"What is it, boy?"

The glare.

"Do you wanna go out?"

The glare.

"Come on, then!"

"Oh yeah!"

Then Theo was his. Away from the chalk and the drone and the gray world that was often part of systems. Into the world of sky, sea, footpaths, and berries. In this way, Shadow served as a charon between the worlds, as all dogs must. Nature's glory is their secret gift. They are unlike the charons of old who row the boats from the world of the living to the world of the dead. Dogs are the *new* charons, oar creatures. They row humankind from the world of civilization to the world of Nature.

When Theo would laugh or guffaw beneath the spreading canopy of Red, Shadow knew he had accomplished his job. The gray mask of civilization had fallen from the boy. Death left his eyes. Blood returned to his cheeks. There was song in his voice. Together, dog and master were once again in the huff and roar of the natural, bliss-filled world. They played ball, Shadow fetched rope, and, weather permitting, they swam in the sea. They proved once more what the ancients knew in the magical first world—that there was peace in play.

Theo took Shadow anywhere and everywhere society allowed. When Theo got his driver's license, his first passenger was Shadow. The dog loved the way Theo drove. He steered right for the potholes, so the old pickup truck could hurl into the air and jolt back onto the road. Shadow barked his joy, yipping a yahoo for more.

Shadow even joined Theo on rides to the Boys Scout troop meetings. From a window outside the Troop Lodge, Shadow watched Theo receive his Eagle Scout badge. Theo stood in the candlelight of the inauguration with the other young men. His golden sash across his chest glittered with achievement medals. Theo had worked hard and for many years. For all his work with the bagpipes, he even got his merit badge in Bugling. Of course, he won his merit badge for Dog Care too. Shadow was so proud of his master standing amidst the flames of the candlewicks. He was certain that Theo, now an eagle, could fly with Thunderbird.

One day, when Theo was at school, Shadow sojourned down Cockle Cove Road and convinced Cleopatra to travel with him. It was one of those brilliant cerulean-blue days. *The sort of blue found in tropical seas,* thought Shadow, *just like on the island in Robinson Crusoe.*

"But where will you take me, my king?" Cleopatra asked in her ancient animal-cant. In the sun, her fur was bone white.

"To see the world," he replied, his tail guilelessly wagging with happiness.

Cleopatra took the leap with Shadow, for she admired his questing for adventure. His encouragement was all she needed to step off familiar ground and travel into the town with all its wondrous mysteries. When cat and dog walked past the boxer's house, Zeus could only snarl.

They traveled the gray-tie tracks of the Old Colony Railroad into the village. A turkey rattled in the bramble. A turtle traipsed into a thicket.

Cleopatra marveled at the red door and the red signage at Kresge's Five and Dime. In all her life, the cat's blue eyes had never seen so much red in one place. She was overwhelmed by the pure white of the library porch. When she skittered up the steps to the porch outside the front door, Shadow was amazed how the cat with bone-white fur disappeared into the sun-blanched white of the temple.

"This could be your hideout," Shadow said, observantly, to Cleopatra. He was so proud of his friend. Unlike Zeus, she had moved beyond the life of mere comfort. She sought understanding through adventuring.

"Can we always be as this?"

"Why not?" answered Shadow. "If we want to, we will be."

"I want to—white against white, hidden from the sorrows, where we can never know hurt."

"The humans call that peace," said Shadow in his animal-cant.

For hours, Cleopatra and Shadow sat on the front porch of the public library, dreaming of peace. Shadow knew he was fortunate for he had largely found that peace with his master—playing ball or telling stories. Just like Theo and Alice, the people would come and go, into and out of the library, taking books in to return and taking books out to read.

"What an odd couple," said Ruth Pullman of Cherry Tree Lane about the tiger-marked dog and the blue-eyed cat sitting together on the top step.

"What could they be talking about?" asked Nancy Foy of Starfish Avenue.

"God only knows," replied Ruth Pullman with a laugh. "God only knows."

CHAPTER FIFTEEN

Shadow's favorite treat was not Cheerios, although he did love Cheerios. It was not beef jerky or even hot milk cake—he had learned his lesson there. Shadow's favorite treat was ice cream. His affection began after Theo introduced him to the cold confection served at Saywells Drugstore when they would share a cone on the bench in the town square.

Things had changed.

Now, Theo drove. He was different when he drove the truck. He was more than a boy. He was a youth. Like a bird who had molted his feathers, he smelled different. His creatureliness gave him a soft down on his upper lip and on his chin. And Shadow? Shadow was now a front-seat dog.

He stuck his head out the window and let the air pour over his fur. The wind whipped his ears against his skull. It was fun. He kept his head straining against the wind for as long as he could stand it.

The two of them needed destinations to which they could go. Theo laughed and sang their song to signal they were on their way.

I scream. You scream. We all scream for ice cream!

Shadow knew very well what that meant.

We're going to Dairy Queen!

Dairy Queen was a nice enough seaside establishment. It distinguished itself from all the other small white clapboard shanties by possessing a giant ice cream cone that seemed to float above the small white hut. Dairy Queen served delicious cones and ice cream bars and was open from April to October.

Each time Shadow and Theo went to the Dairy Queen, they shared a delicious vanilla cone dipped in a strawberry shell. Theo preferred chocolate, but most dogs were allergic to it. Some were known to even die from it. It was fun to share a cone, for the hard strawberry would crack and the ice cream would drip into the breaks and you had to lick fast or the ice cream would fall to the ground.

When Alice learned of the cone-sharing, she said, "That is awful! That is disgusting!"

"Aww, come on, Mom, Shadow loves it."

"It's not sanitary!"

"It is a scientific fact that dogs have cleaner mouths than humans."

"I have seen Shadow eat dog poop!"

Theo thought about this. Just to be safe, and just to be a good friend to Shadow, Theo began to buy two single vanilla cones with strawberry dip, rather than one double.

"Now we both have one, sport," Theo said as he sat on the outdoor picnic bench at the Dairy Queen while he held Shadow's cone in one hand and his in the other.

Shadow sat beside Theo until his ice cream was almost finished. Then, Theo dropped the remaining cone at the side of the picnic table, and Shadow wolfed it down in the grass.

Eventually, as it came to all New England, the frost would come to the Dairy Queen. In October, the screen doors were replaced by shutters. In November, the place closed for the season. The winter came. The charcoal winds blew cold. It was hot cocoa and hot soup until the birds returned in spring.

In April of 1951 the Dairy Queen expanded to three times its size. Gone was the little order and pick-up window that Theo and Shadow had known. No longer was there simply ice cream and Cokes. Now, there were burgers, hotdogs, and *fries*. Even ice cream shops arrived at the Atomic Age. Shadow licked his mouth with his tongue as soon as he saw the Diary Queen sign.

Most importantly for Theo, a circular parking lot surrounded the new building. Here, cars parked. Girls in starched white caps and rocket-red lipstick zoomed to your car window on roller skates. They collected your order and delivered the goods right to your car window.

"We now stay in the car to eat the cone, Shadow. That's how it's done in the modern world. Do you understand?" Theo said.

Yippee, Shadow replied. He could barely get the word out as he was so busy licking his mouth.

"Which means, of course, we can't drop the last part of the cone onto the floor to eat it. It's gonna get sticky down there fast. You have to finish the cone from my hand. Do you understand?"

Yippee, Shadow replied.

After a few weeks, Shadow noticed that Theo's preferred parking spots at the Dairy Queen were R, S, T, U, or V.

In fact, sometimes the pickup truck would wait under the big green maple tree until one of those five spots would become available. There were other girls who would come to the window, but Shadow noticed there was a special girl in a starched white cap and that is why Theo waited.

Theo would smooth his brown hair in the mirror with spit and a comb from his back pocket. His hair always looked shiny and sorted before he pulled the truck into the spot.

He never really spoke to the girl with the chestnut hair and the blue eyes. Theo simply ordered and said thank you. But Shadow knew that this day was special. It was crowded at the Dairy Queen, so Theo had to wait with his truck under the maple tree for quite some time before he could park in space R. Through the windshield, Shadow watched the gray squirrels flashing through the branches of the maple. He wanted to pounce, but he knew to respect whatever his master was experiencing. Theo put his hands together and whispered a prayer. "You have to ask for it," Theo told Shadow. "Magic doesn't come unless it's summoned." He moved his car into drive when R became available.

"I'm Theo Snow," he said to the girl.

"I know who you are," the girl with blue eyes and pink eye shadow said. "You're the two-single-vanilla-cones-strawberry-dip guy. One for you and the other for your hairy date."

Yippee, Shadow barked as the pretty girl acknowledged him.

"You're a sassy one, aren't you?" Theo asked.

"The usual?" she asked, ignoring his question.

"The usual," he answered.

When she glided away on her roller skates, also rocket-red with silver lightning bolts, Theo turned to Shadow.

"I like sassy, don't you?" Theo asked.

Shadow barked enthusiastically.

Theo swallowed. His mouth was dry.

Theo cast his emerald eyes back to the girl at the order window. He could hardly breathe. Her radiance was as inescapable as the sun. Love is never stronger than the love in the young. There, love is unreasonable and preposterous and beautiful. Theo did not realize it at the time, but his young self was dying inside to the man he would become.

Any boy or man who has loved understands the force found in those three ordinary letters that form the idea—*she*. Theo loved the idea of *she*. Lora Landis became his new destination. It would take a man to sail to her distant blue. Now, he bore the compass. Later, when they first held each other, breast to breast, she bent toward him, her chestnut hair brushing his cheek, leaving it aflame. Wing to wing. Fire to fire. *She*.

CHAPTER SIXTEEN

They had never been apart. Theo explained why he needed to get educated and go away for a while. He took his footballs, his rucksack, and his clothes, but he left Shadow behind. With Theo gone, Shadow walked about the kitchen. Every step revealed his listlessness. He could not eat. When he did, he vomited up his food. He lost weight.

"Theo went to learn how to care for sick animals," Alice explained to Shadow.

"Doesn't he know that, without him, I am the one who is sick?" Shadow asked in his animal-cant.

But he did not know whether Alice understood the low whine in his throat, for his question went unanswered. Day after day, the teeth of his query raked his mind and heart into a gray loneliness.

"All big boys grow up," said Alice as she and Shadow walked the ebbing tides of Cockle Cove Beach. Water pearled past Shadow's paws. "And then, if they are fortunate," Alice said, "they have boys and girls of their own."

Shadow listened to Alice's soothing voice. He was *really* listening. It was clear to Shadow that Alice missed Theo too. With Ted buried and Theo in another land, she had no one but Shadow.

Shadow stayed close to Alice. He knew that both Thunderbird and Mother wanted that for him. It was not his will. It was his duty to the stars. Shadow did love the woman, but it was just not the same without his Theo. Alice, too, knew his grief. In fact, she shared it with him. There was comfort in the collective abandonment both male and female possessed when their baby left them behind to pursue the bigger worlds.

For the first month or so, Alice kept Theo's room open, and the dog slept on Theo's bed. He lay in the imprint Theo's body had made in the mattress after all those years. Shadow thought by dreaming about him the dreams would bring him back. But the dog found that the dreams did not. When he heard Alice cry one night, Shadow leapt from Theo's bed, nosed open the door, walked down the hallway, and entered Alice's room.

Alice still had the same bed as the one Ted and she had shared when Ted was alive. He realized that Alice was only having a nightmare. He quietly walked over to her and licked the unsettled hand that hung over the side of the bed until she awoke.

"Oh, you are such a good boy," she mumbled to him.

He did not know why, for it was not his place, but he raised his two paws onto her mattress. He raised his homesick eyes to her.

"Do you want to come up, boy?" she asked.

That was all he needed to hear. She was as close to his home as possible.

Shadow bounded onto the bed and sunk into the large mattress. It was much softer than Theo's. He did not know why, but he sensed Alice was cold. He went to her side and laid "taco" style next to her.

She patted his belly. He could feel the sadness in her palm. That night in the comfy bed, he came to the truth that roiled the cosmos—people missed other people as much as dogs did.

When the leaves turned red and dropped from their branches, the fires became more plentiful in the house. Alice told Shadow the fall light was good light, bright and crisp.

Yippee, Shadow replied for he loved the autumn too.

The ropy char-smoke of the bonfires filled his nostrils with delicious, dense fragrances. The dry ache of the strewn corn husks sang the nearness of winter. The brick chimneys of the house swelled in heat.

"What do you say you and I paint a picture for Theo for Christmas? That way, he will always remember us."

Yippee, Shadow barked as he liked that idea as much as Mom did.

"I know the perfect picture," she said. "Wait right here, boy."

Shadow sat patiently in the studio. Alice came back with a large cardboard box. She sat down in the sunshine-filled room next to Shadow. She opened the carton filled with photographs. They were little pieces of time captured by cameras. Shadow had a good memory, but it was often triggered more deeply when he saw the framed photos on the side tables and mantels.

Shadow was happy to report he could be found in many of the photos. He was right there amongst the prints of the New

England painters Alice adored—N. C. Wyeth, Edward Hopper, Grant Wood, Winslow Homer, and Thomas Hart Benton.

Alice placed the photos from the box on the floor, hunting for just the right piece of time. Shadow looked at the pictures of his boy—at football practice, wearing his play stethoscope, holding hands with the sparkly-eyed Dairy Queen girl the night of the high school prom.

He noticed the pictures of Ted—some bright after his re-form, others dark and filled with violence.

Shadow sniffed the chemicals and dust on the pictures until Alice said, "Aha. I think I have it, boy!"

She held out the photograph. It was of Shadow and Alice sitting under the Christmas tree. Alice wore a sweater and a strand of pearls. Shadow remembered that Christmas Day. Theo took the picture with his first Brownie camera.

O' the boy loved that camera!

When Theo picked his developed roll up at Saywells Drug-store, he looked at that picture and was thrilled.

"What do you think, Shadow?" Alice said with a smile.

Yippee, barked Shadow.

"Do you think he will like it if I turn this into an oil painting?" Alice asked.

Yippee.

Over the next six weeks between Halloween and Christmas, Shadow sat or lay at Alice's feet as she worked. He watched as the portrait took on life in another form—of he and Mom in oil. He marveled at the myriad of brushstrokes, layer after layer becoming a discernable image of himself. He was as royal as Cleopatra viewed him. There sat the King of Sea and

Sky with four good legs with the Queen of Blueberry Hill.

The painting was big and splendid. It was not exactly the way life was. It was the way life should be. Alice wanted to forever freeze this piece of time.

Time passes.

Come closer.

Time passes.

Hurry.

Touch eternity.

"What else could a boy need?" Alice said one day as she looked at the painting emerging from the canvas. "A dog and his mom? Is this not enough?" she asked Shadow. But the dog did not yippee.

Shadow knew that his big boy who left also needed more.

Lora Landis, the girl with pink eye shadow from the Dairy Queen, would come over on Sundays from time to time as she was not going to school in a place called Boston. She always brought Shadow treats. The creamier the better. He loved the frosted cranberry surprise. "Here you go, my hedonist," she said as he smiled his smile. Lora was at a community college where she was studying to be a nurse. "I'm swapping one white cap for another," she told Alice as they sipped on wonderful-smelling coffee in the kitchen.

Shadow always lay at Alice or Lora's feet, blissful with the hot aromas steaming from their teacups. Lora soon learned to make him his favorite—buttered toast. When the Sunbeam toaster popped, Shadow's ears thundered with excitement.

Sometimes, the women would walk together on the beach with Shadow. Sojourning with them reminded Shadow of his walks with Theo. Often, he sensed Theo in pace with the three of them, walking as a single family through the lacey froth of the ebbing tides.

Other times, Lora would bring over a new "soundtrack" album. Shadow loved music and enjoyed it when Alice would put records on the hi-fi. When the strings and flutes played, Shadow had no fear. Shadow was invulnerable.

"What's a nurse doing with this massive opera collection?" Alice had said with a smile as they listened to "Figaro's Aria" from The Barber of Seville.

"No one is just one thing, Alice. I am not just a nurse," she said. "I love music. I have been singing mezzo-soprano in the choir since I was ten years old."

Lora also had albums of hit American musicals including Carousel, South Pacific, and The Pajama Game. When Shadow heard the song from Carousel, it reminded him of he and Theo.

> When you walk through a storm, hold your head up high
> And don't be afraid of the dark
> At the end of the storm, there's a golden sky
> And the sweet, silver song of a lark
> Walk on through the wind
> Walk on through the rain
> Though your dreams be tossed and blown
> Walk on, walk on
> With hope in your heart
> And you'll never walk alone
> You'll never walk alone

"I am trying to teach Theo to become an opera lover. Opera is so expansive, filled with such drama and joy," Lora said.

"Anything is possible when love is involved, even Theo liking opera," Alice said with a laugh. Then, Alice's green eyes ballooned as if she suddenly realized something. "You do love him, don't you, Lora?"

"Oh, I do, Alice," Lora said.

Shadow enjoyed the easy, sweet Sunday life of the farmhouse when the two women traded stories and song. Coffee and cream. Laughter and tears. He liked Lora. She brought him creamy treats, not the dry stuff. And when she laughed at his snoring underneath the table, she would awaken him so he would not miss any of the action. He enjoyed this matriarchate much more than Ted's rough reign. Sometimes, lying at the feet of Lora and Alice, on the cool kitchen floor, Shadow dreamed. He dreamed of the ancient times when tribal mothers ruled. Men hunted, but it was the women who shaped the wolves and the babies by the ring of fire into magic dogs and magic men.

Shadow was amazed when an electric box came into the great room of the house. It told stories, just like the Star Raider radio. But the stories included pictures!

Now Ozzie, Harriet, David, and Ricky were no longer simply voices. *They all had faces and arms and legs!*

For the first time, Shadow could actually see Ozzie and Harriet. Lora often came on Sunday nights and watched the television magic with Alice and Shadow.

Most of the shows were funny. Shadow knew this because the two ladies would laugh at *I Love Lucy* and *Make Room for Daddy.*

When Theo came back from college for Christmas break,

Shadow was astonished. His heart quickened as Theo stepped out of the truck. His white paws beat against the wooden planks of the kitchen floor like battering batons on a parade drum. His tail shot up in fever. He was all waggery.

Theo climbed the steps to the porch as Shadow, his wide mouth in a laugh shape, pushed the kitchen door open and rushed him. He jumped him with such happy fury, Theo had to drop his duffle bag in order not to fall. He kissed and slobbered on Theo in a hundred ways on his face and neck. He licked and sniffed the shoulders and sleeves of his blue pea coat.

Theo called him the ol' kissing monster.

"Oh, I have missed you, boy," Theo said as he sat at the foot of the Christmas tree and hugged Shadow. The dog was all lazy and content. In the firelight, he yawned and groaned with the ecstatic purring of a tiger. "You made me wise before my time," said Theo.

During the winter break, Shadow and Theo took walks together while the bone-white gulls flew above them, with Lora mostly by their sides. The foot paths had dried in the cold, cracking into star patterns. Shadow was patient as Theo and Lora hugged and kissed and played roughhouse. He liked Lora. She was kind to him and brought him wet treats as well as Cheerios. She let him eat from her finished plate. He had no problem sharing Theo with Lora. Shadow discovered when there was love, there was always plenty to go around.

On Christmas morning, Theo opened Alice's gift. He was thrilled with the painting of Shadow and his mother. He hugged his mom and tousled Shadow's fur saying what a good boy he was for selecting that photograph for the painting.

"I will take this everywhere I go. I'm taking it back to the dorm even if the frame is a little fancy. Not that I ever need anything to remind me of my two best friends."

Then he took both the dog and his mom into his arms for a family hug.

In the evening, Shadow slept in the kitchen by the fire. He faked it by keeping his eyes closed when Alice or Theo would lumber off to bed.

He did not want Alice to believe that he was showing favorites by sleeping in Theo's room, and he wanted Theo to know that he, too, could be a "big boy" and sleep alone without him.

He could be his own taco.

But such fakery was hard. Still, as hard as it was, he knew that Theo would be leaving him soon enough, and he did not want to become too comfortable with the heat of the boy's creatureliness.

That was the way it was.

It was not enough for any big-boy human just to have a dog and a mom.

So, Shadow accepted it when Theo and Lora went off skiing to Stowe, Vermont for the new year. In fact, he was happy for them even though he missed both of them terribly.

But Shadow had his memories. Shadow had his dreams. The boy needed more. But for Shadow, he had enough. His master's hands no longer smelled of mud and hamburger patties and potatoes and sweat and sugar. They smelled of soap and typewriter ribbons and fresh paper. Later, Theo smelled of chemicals and animals and soap, for he was to become a doctor in animal medicine.

Theo returned to college.

Life moved on.

For some, being a vet was a means to make a living. For Theo, helping animals was a photo of his soul, the coat of his will.

CHAPTER SEVENTEEN

When it was time for Theo and Lora to become "serious," well even more serious than they had always been to one another, Shadow was there for the important milestones. Lora had become close to Shadow in Theo's absence. Indeed, both Alice and Lora found a remnant of Theo in Shadow—his enthusiasms, his friendliness, his want to love.

"You are my church," Lora told Shadow one day.

Shadow could not understand how he was a building with a bell and an ecclesiastical steeple. However, he did love the songs of prayer that rose from the people when they sang of their god's glory at the church with the old mast.

Even with Theo coming and going with the dropping and lifting of his rucksacks, Lora was always there. Like Alice.

She came by foot, by car, in fancy pink dresses and khaki shorts and hiking boots. She told Shadow she had once had a dog, Domino. He was a Dalmatian who had grown up with her. They, too, took walks and runs and played chase and fetch. He loved dog biscuits. But, she explained, he had never known the secrets of Cheerios.

Domino was hit by a car on Main Street when Lora was

just ten years old. Her family buried Domino in the back yard.

She confided in Shadow that she dressed up as a nun for the funeral. She had just seen Jennifer Jones in the *Song of Bernadette*. She longed to be devout like Jennifer.

Lora and her mom sang Christmas carols over the grave. She and her dad planted a rhododendron on Domino's burial plot.

According to Lora, the flowering shrub has bloomed ever since with delicate flutes of red and pink petals.

"I want to become petals too," Shadow told her in his venerable language. He was sure that she understood for she petted his crown as he held the thought.

When Theo came home from veterinarian college, he looked more like his father, Ted, than the boy Shadow had grown up to guide and to love. Theo was tall. He shaved so his whiskers would not become a beard. His shoulders had grown wide. Even his voice sounded different. It was less like a lark. More like a goose. Yet, his breath still bore the same sweetness. Shadow was not concerned that he resembled the assaulter. For when Theo drew near and whispered in his ear "How ya doin'?" or "How are the tricks?" the man was still the boy who had once made a room for him out of a firewood closet. Theo was his life and would always be his life. Even though he was away from him for so long, they were together in spirit. Even as they sojourned on different roads, they walked side by side.

> Walk on through the wind
> Walk on through the rain
> Though your dreams be tossed and blown
> Walk on, walk on
> With hope in your heart
> And you'll never walk alone
> You'll never walk alone

In the summer, there was not only the Dairy Queen, but a new creation—drive-in movies! These were stories with pictures just like television. But the screens were so big you could not watch them except outside, and the stories were in color! Theo would pull the pickup truck through a red, white, and blue arch where a man would open a long gate. Theo parked the truck with he and Lora inside. Sometimes, Shadow got to be a front-seat dog, but more often, he sat in the bed of the truck to watch. He leaned out from the bed of the truck, or sometimes, he even climbed on the cab of the pickup to watch.

There were wonderful stories in those summers in the 1950s.

The screens shimmered with glittering giant humans called "stars." Some of Shadow's favorite stories included *Roman Holiday*, *Peter Pan*, and *The Seven Year Itch*. *The Seven Year Itch* reminded Shadow that people could be very, very silly.

He loved the wonderful cartoons from a man named Walt Disney. He liked the animal cartoons best: *Dumbo* and *Bambi*. He wondered if Ted, when he drank, saw "Pink Elephants on Parade" like Dumbo and the crow when they had too much to drink. But his favorite was *Lady and the Tramp*.

He got to sit in the front seat for that one. It was the story of an uptown cocker spaniel, Lady, and a trashy but nice alley mutt who was named Tramp. It was a love story, but Shadow did not really know that kind of love.

The closest thing Shadow reckoned to that kind of love was his friendship with Cleopatra. But she was a cat, and he was a dog. That's the way some sad love is—unrequited.

There was one movie that Shadow watched that left him feeling dark and sad. People spoke funny as it was in *Italian*, and there were lots of words at the bottom of the screen. It was called *La Strada*. Theo told him it was "symbolic." *La Strada* meant "the road." There was a muscleman named Zampano who traveled around and broke steel chains by puffing up his chest. He bought a woman with real Italian money. Her name was Gelsomina. She became a clown and helped him in his muscleman show.

Like *Lady and the Tramp*, *La Strada* was also a romance, but it did not end well.

Zampano was mean to Gelsomina and treated her like a slave. He loved other women, not just her. When the little clown-woman died, Zampano went to the sea. He fell into the tide. He clutched the sand and sea in his fists and wept. But he was still mean and did not know how to remove the darkness from himself.

When the movie was over, Theo just stared at the windshield. He did not start the truck so that they could all go for a truck ride.

"What's wrong, Theo?" Lora asked.

"Zampano. He was my father," Theo replied, staring into the distance.

"I am sorry, Theo," she said, gently taking his hand from the steering wheel.

"I just want you to know that I would never ever treat you that way, Lora. I promise you."

"I know, Theo," Lora said gently. "To you, all women are goddesses."

"Lora, I don't want to adore you like some goddess. I want to love you," Theo said. He finally turned to her, looking into her blue eyes. "I love you, Lora." She reached over Shadow and kissed Theo for on that night of *La Strada*, Shadow was a front-seat dog.

"I love you, Theo."

They kissed and hugged and played roughhouse. Whenever love was mentioned, roughhouse was generally forthcoming, at least as far as Shadow could tell. Oftentimes, Shadow jumped in as it was so much fun. He nuzzled his cold nose between their two hot faces and smothered them both with kisses. They laughed and kissed him back. But tonight, in the truck, he chose not to.

There was something sacred going on, just like when the people came in and out of the temple of reading known as the library. He felt the holiness of monks he had seen in *National Geographic* magazine.

Theo had made an oath to Lora to never hurt her.

That was a holy oath.

It was then that Shadow looked out at the new moon. In that moment, even though he was only nine years old, he was already becoming wise. Shadow realized he had found true meaning in his life. He was not a stranger any longer in this strange world.

At that point, he realized he had guided a boy to the kindness of his manhood.

Then Theo turned on the motor, and they went on the truck ride away from the drive-in movie.

"I think I need Shadow to witness this," said Theo as they topped the bluff at Cockle Cove. Lora, Theo, and Shadow looked at the ocean, sun-kissed gold in the descending sun. It was late. A gigantic July sun still shimmered, but the tourists had largely departed the beach for the day. Fireflies flicked their light into the long darkening sea grass.

"Run, boy, run," Theo shouted. The golden king bounded down the golden sand to his golden throne where the ocean met the land. The dog had assimilated his suffering into a healthy new spirit. It was almost impossible to believe Shadow's fourth leg was absent.

Shadow leaped as the ocean's voltage ignited his golden robe of fur. He was so golden it was as if he had swallowed the sun. When the King of Sea and Sky finished dancing, he wandered back to Theo and Lora, becoming their dog again.

The two humans sat on dry shore, watching the tide ebb into the bright, enameled sea. Shadow always gave his wet fur a good shake or two before he came upon Theo and Lora.

For some reason, they preferred his fur dry. Just as they preferred to sit on dry sand or rock. Humans were odd, but he loved their peculiar ways. He had grown accustomed to them. Why they constantly needed to change their faces and hair and clothes was something he could not fathom. But that appeared to be the only permanent thing in life for humans—change.

Why do they do that to themselves? Or do they not have a choice in the matter? Change of clothes. Change of season. Change of scenery.

The only thing that did not seem to change, at least from Shadow's vantage point, was their discernable essence. Something at their core that distinguished them.

Shadow listened to the humans as they sat in the sand and watched the orange ball of sun slowly disappear behind the sparkling waves. Theo reminisced. He told Lora about the alarm clock's silver hand that lodged one night in Shadow's mouth.

That was the beginning of his journey to become a vet.

"I wish you had been around when Domino got hit. Maybe you could have saved him," Lora said.

"Do you think that is why you became a nurse?" Theo asked. "Because of Domino?"

"I never thought of it. I suppose that might have something to do with it. I know we can never end all the suffering here, but we can lend a helping hand," she replied.

"I would like to be your helping hand," Theo said. Shadow watched as Lora took Theo's hand up to her lips and kissed his fingers.

Theo took out a small box that opened like a clamshell. Inside, an ancient stone from Mother Earth shined.

"I would like to be yours as well," she said as she stared at him and the stone.

He placed the ancient stone on her finger. It was the symbol of a love that would always be.

In the days ahead, Shadow overheard them talk with Alice on the front porch.

Boxes and trunks and duffel bags returned from the land of college to the farmhouse at Blueberry Hill.

Shadow was thrilled.

Theo was staying "for good."

Yippee.

He was going to marry Lora, and they were all going to move back into the house. Shadow pushed around Theo's old football, which he had brought back from college. He had not seen that in years.

"Hullo, Ball," Shadow *yippeed* as he pounced on it.

The ball was silent, as always. But Shadow was so excited about the news that Theo was coming home, he ran around all of Blueberry Hill with the football.

Shadow heard that Dr. Cook had waited one extra year for Theo to finish school before retiring. This way the small town would always have a veterinarian and Theo could inherit the practice from his mentor and friend. The farmhouse was going to be reorganized too. Theo and Lora would re-wallpaper the big bedroom where Alice and Ted used to sleep. Alice would move into the second-floor sewing room. That would become her bedroom.

Theo and Shadow's room would become a nursery, whatever that was. But Shadow did recall nursing on his mother's teats when he was just a pup. He found that highly comforting. He agreed there should be more nursing on Blueberry Hill if new puppies showed up.

"And you, my man?" said Theo as he sat with Shadow in the kitchen and scratched underneath his chin. "You can sleep wherever you want to. You can sleep with Mom or with Lora and I or you can even sleep with the new baby when he or she is old enough, provided we are blessed to have one."

Shadow barked with approval. Theo had wiped away his guilt and shame. He sometimes felt guilty for tacoing with mom. Sometimes, he was sad when he tacoed with Theo because, then, Alice was all alone. But now Theo had figured it out for him!

I can sleep anywhere!

I can taco with everyone!

Shadow was so happy with the good news he careened through the house, slipping on the waxed wooden floors in the kitchen and hallways, jumping into the soft carpets of the bedrooms, and battering his white paws against the ground just like Ahanu had once beat his ceremonial drums. *O' tomorrow, how wonderful it all will be!* He even treated himself to a cool drink of water from the toilet bowl.

"You're the man of the house, now, Shadow," said Theo. "Rule us with a gentle touch," he said as he threw a baseball across the yard. Shadow caught it.

When Theo explained to Shadow that he was going to be the best man at his wedding, there was nothing that Shadow could do but agree. Theo explained that Ted was gone, and Tyler Eiger was deployed. Tyler could not return for the wedding. Shadow could not understand about the war games that humans played.

When they roughhoused, they killed each other.

Why can't they just roughhouse like dogs, and when they are through, walk away?

So it was that Shadow found himself in the front seat of the new station wagon that Theo had bought after he finished all those years in college land. It was called a woody wagon. It had real wood on the sides.

Shadow was not permitted to chew on the wood.

Unlike the pickup truck, Shadow was now required to have a towel underneath him. "They are new seats, and I intend to keep them that way. It's not like that nasty old pickup truck," Theo said.

Shadow did not really care about nasty or new. He was simply happy when he could stick his nose out of a car window and feel the rush of wind on his eyes and fur.

Riding in the woody wagon with his head out the window wasn't quite like romping at the ocean, but it was heaven on earth, nonetheless, even with the towel over the seats.

Heaven was with Shadow now. There was no need to want for heaven anymore. It was not only above his head in the soaring wagon, but it was also running in the earth beneath the wheels. There can be no life unless we are awake to it. There can be no heaven nor hell unless we open our eyes to it. Shadow was awake and alive to the spirited adventure known as his life.

At the fancy Gray Colt Haberdashers, Theo took Shadow to buy a bow tie. The establishment smelled of leather, cotton, and shoe polish.

"He already has a tuxedo with that fur," Theo said

"Oh, I can see that," replied the salesman. "He is quite majestic I should say." Indeed, he was as majestic as any king should be. In Shadow's advancing years, he had grown into the sage-king. His body had filled out. He was strong. The white scruff about his neck had grown thicker, longer like the mane of a lion enjoying his prime.

"But he needs a proper bow tie," said Theo. "He's going to be the best man at my wedding this Saturday."

"Well, then, this dog needs to be properly attired," said the salesman with enthusiasm. "A top hat too?"

"No top hat," answered Theo. Shadow battered his paws on the floor in agreement.

Shadow thought wearing a bowtie was rather like wearing a collar, which he didn't mind much. He didn't fidget when the salesman put the black bowtie around the mane of his neck. Theo and he walked to a floor mirror. Theo knelt on the carpet and examined his best man, who stared with him into the reflection. The satin black tie fit nicely on his white-golden neck. It could be easily seen when he was in a sitting position.

Of course, it could not be seen at all when he was walking.

"Shadow makes a handsome best man," said the salesman.

"He's a good-looking boy," replied Theo. Shadow knew better than to bark in agreement, especially at such a fancy-schmancy shop with the shoe-polish smell. Outside the shop, for being such a good boy, Theo rewarded his dog with Cheerios from his pocket.

With all this talk of being a best man and a good boy, Shadow was primed with pride. When he and Theo rode back to the farm, he could not wait to pee upon every marker on the farm. After all, there was a wedding happening on the hill, and everyone needed to know who reigned over wedding land. That included Zeus. Even though he wasn't invited. That also included those unmannered magpies from Emmett Bluff.

The wedding on Blueberry Hill was an autumn wedding. In the fields, the corn stood tall and thick, it's golden meat bursting against its own green husks. Just like Theo's birthday all those years ago, there were spheres of color that floated into the day in pink and purple and white. The star-shaped leaves of the sweetgum tree were radiant red. There was a massive tiered cake, which was for humans only.

Shadow greeted all the guests to his kingdom. He was proud of his special bowtie. As the milkweed pods burst in the distant fields, Shadow sat beside a huge willow basket teeming with flowers at the end of the driveway.

As instructed, Shadow sat with friendly eyes and nosed the guests as they passed him, giving each of them a sunflower from Alice's garden. Shadow received hundreds of pats on his head for being sweet and so intelligent.

We are intelligent, he thought. *Since I am a dog, my intelligence plays just as much a part in me as my nature.*

He wanted to lie down for an occasional tummy rub, especially when Ahanu and Oota Dabun arrived. They knew how
to rub him just the right way, especially Oota. He had been
told "absolutely not" by his master several times. This was a
formal affair.

Everyone smiled when Shadow walked down the little aisle
laden with sunflowers. Even Reverend Cummings from the
church enjoyed a chortle. Shadow wore a small leather box
tied on his back. That box held an ancient circle of belonging.
Of belonging together. To one another.

Shadow listened while Lora, in a fluffy white dress, and
Theo, in a bow tie, had a holy conversation at the front of the
aisle with the reverend. At the appropriate time, Shadow held
his back straight as Theo took the box from Shadow's back.

Theo opened the clamshell box and pulled out the circle
from its purple-velvet bed. As Shadow sat on his haunches,
he watched in wonder as the silver circle glimmered in a sunbeam.

When Theo placed the ring on Lora's finger, Shadow could
not help thinking this event was as sacred as going to the
public library. Soon, there was kissing, a little wrestling, and
lots of applause as Lora and Theo finished their conversation
under an arbor of flowers.

At the reception that was held outdoors at the top of the
hill, Theo played "Amazing Grace" on the bagpipes. Lora, Alice,
and Shadow did a circle-dance together while Theo played.
The three of them gamboled on the portable floor that had
been erected and brought in all the way from Hartford. Shadow did well on one leg, while each woman held one of his
front paws. Shadow could not really understand why everyone
at the wedding cried at the end of the bagpipe dance. A wedding was a blissful event. He thought it must have something
to do with the bagpipes. Theo had always told Shadow that

he would be a "hit" at baptisms, weddings, and funerals if he mastered the playing of "Amazing Grace."

If tears were any indication, Theo must have been a "hit."

Shadow sat beside Alice at a table as she stroked his golden crown. They looked out at the dance floor and watched Lora and Theo dance to "Rock Around the Clock."

Shadow felt the cadence of Alice's blood thrumming through her gentle hand. He looked up at the mother. He saw her eyes shining wet.

"We did it, boy," she said. Her words pricked his ears. He watched her radiant smile.

"Theo is a lover," she whispered.

Shadow understood. Yes, he thought. *There is the boy, happy and gentle and grown.* He was sweet with Lora, and he was strong. He witnessed, from their bones, the immense angel they had constructed while they danced. Their wings were as wide as the wings of Thunderbird. As Alice's fingers thrummed with her music across his head, Shadow, too, found himself caught in the high, old way of love.

Lora and Theo went away for a while. Shadow missed them. When they came back, they had tan faces and wore shorts even though it was almost Thanksgiving.

Lora stayed over more. Also, when Lora and Theo had roughhouse at night, they took off all their clothes. Theo even took off his eyeglasses. Theo was very white. Lora was very pink.

The wrestling, sometimes, went on and on.

Shadow would get bored because he was not allowed to play with them. They were always nice and happy when they shooed him away, but they shooed him away, nonetheless. Shadow figured he did not have the right coat of skin. Shadow's coat was furry, not smooth. Plus, he had no way of taking off his coat, like the humans did when they shed their dresses and shirts.

He realized this sort of wrestling wasn't for him, so he would lie down in the corner of the room for there was no cubby now in the big room.

He would go taco with Alice or lie down in the kitchen. The fire there would be warm, and the wooden floor would be cool. He would lie with his paws in the air. He liked to sleep on something cool. As he got older, Shadow liked that a lot.

Shadow also enjoyed lying on the chilly white tile of the bathroom while Lora sang opera in the shower. She sang with bliss. It was contagious. While he would not howl along with her, his tail would wag uncontrollably as she warbled. She sang in a different language. It was called Italian just like those words in the *La Strada* movie.

She continued to sing as she stepped out of the shower. Shadow loved to sniff all the lovely scents and powders she rubbed over her pink body. Like Theo, Lora let Shadow lick her ankles with his rough tongue whenever he was compelled. She giggled, ticklish. He loved her soapy, salty skin.

When Lora got a big stomach, Shadow was put in charge of the baby's room. The workmen came and stripped away the wallpaper of the many Supermans. Even with only three legs, Shadow took the boxes of old wallpaper down the stairs, walked through the kitchen, and placed them in the garbage at the back of the new red barn.

Shadow knew he would miss all the Supermans. But he

understood one of the important lessons of his life—what was gone from reality was not absent from the heart.

Superman will always remain within me and the boy.

The workmen were impressed with Shadow's ability to help haul paper to the backyard. Nonetheless, there were no treats for him. Just "good boys" and pats on his head, which were enough for Shadow.

If the workmen move in, there will need to be treats, thought Shadow. *After all, I am King of Sea and Sky.*

Theo sanded down the empty nursery with an electric sander from Sears. Shadow was a little sad as he remembered the reliquary of toys that had once filled it when he first moved in to the cubby—the wooden boat, the metal Ferris wheel, all the rubber balls too numerous to count. He even recalled the book of human wisdom—*The Puppy Book.* They had all been moved to a land of exile known as the attic.

Once the bedroom walls were smooth, Theo painted the room white. When Theo was finished, the room was so bright that Shadow squinted from its glow.

Sometimes, Shadow lay in the white room on the cool wooden floor and felt Thunderbird fly with him as he dreamed about the new child who would sleep and grow in this room. That child would have children and they would have children and the arc of humanity would not dim. This was life. It goes on. Such dreams filled Shadow with adventurous hope, as much as Theo's stories of *Huckleberry Finn* and *Lassie.*

New England men and woman loved their stenciling. When it came time to "finish" the room, Alice brought a bucket load of large stencils for Shadow to review.

There were all kinds of animals—beautiful beasts that Shadow had never met personally but had seen plenty of times on the television Nature shows. There were insects too—beetles, butterflies, and honeybees.

As Alice held them up for him to consider, Shadow barked with approval. He liked almost all animals and barked enthusiastically for the regal silhouettes of elephants, bears, lions, rhinos, and, of course, dogs. He was silent on squirrels, snakes, and mice, having certain concerns toward them. Consequently, they did not earn a place on the wall.

Shadow encouraged Alice with the stenciling by laying at her feet. When she had to climb the step ladder to reach the ceiling with an elephant ear or a giraffe's head, Shadow would steady the ladder by laying his body across the lowest rung, just like he had done for Theo when he painted the house.

"What a good boy you are," said Alice of his work.

Theo and Lora were delighted with all the animals in the nursery.

When it came to another Thanksgiving, Shadow lay at Lora's feet as the family said their prayers of gratitude before they ate turkey and chestnut stuffing and green beans and pumpkin pie. He loved Thanksgiving, for there were always wonderful smells lifting the house toward heaven. After the feast was over, for several days in a row, Shadow received his favorite meal in his supper bowl—turkey sandwiches and chestnut stuffing.

The Saturday after Thanksgiving, Theo took Shadow for a ride to show him his new office. It was in the center of town, in between Saywells Drugstore and the Windjammer Bar. It was a storefront office with a blue door, the same azure blue as the shutters of the farmhouse. Shadow knew the building well, for it had been Dr. Cook's clinic. There, he received many small stings over his lifetime from the vet with the round spectacles.

In the waiting area, the framed oil of Alice and Shadow hung above the magazine table that included a pile of *Life* and *Look* magazines, and of course, Shadow's favorite, *National Geographic*.

A large African mask of the lion, the king of all beasts, hung in the foyer outside the back alley. Alice had painted the mask, too, in a blaze of bright primary colors for Theo's new business.

In the alley at the back of his office on Main Street, Theo attended to the animals too large or unruly for the front door: horses, cows, bulls, and even llamas. Saturday was alley day, so Shadow sat patiently on the door stoop as one trailer after another came and went, carrying all kinds of wonderful beasts who just needed a little gentle aid from his master.

The King of Sea and Sky was proud of Theo's mastery. Being a novice was safe. When you are learning how to do something, you do not have to worry about whether or not you are good at it. But when you have done something, have learned how to do it again, you are not safe anymore. Being a master opens you up to judgment. Shadow wagged his tail in happy judgment to see the cheer in his master's blissful face as he hopped from one trailer to the next.

On the wall next to Theo's desk hung a still life Alice had painted. It was a rendering of the alarm clock of Shadow's youth. The silver clock hands had been pulled. They lay on the table in the painting. The still life wore a small bronze plaque with the inscription, What Dogs Do.

Inevitably, the conversation with a client would roll around to the question of what dogs did. Theo would look at the broken clock hanging on the wall. His eyes twinkled. He would wax on like a young philosopher who had read the collected works of Thoreau and Emerson. Of course, he had read all the books of the temple.

"Have you ever walked with your dog on a summer's morning on the seashore? Or walked with him on an autumn's afternoon when the leaves are in full color?"

Inevitably, the client would say yes.

"And did it sometimes feel that all of Nature was your own room? That you could be there forever?"

"Yes."

"Well, that's what dogs do. They destroy time."

"Ah," they inevitably said. They destroy time—nodding their heads.

As they were dog guys and dog gals, they understood.

Time passes.

Come closer.

Time passes.

Hurry.

Touch eternity.

Shadow was impressed with the office. It was the way Theo dreamed it would be all those years ago while sitting on a fallen tree in the salt marsh when Shadow and he were both small. Shadow finally understood something about human bliss. He could see how happy Theo was as he showed him all around the office. Shadow knew then that the truest life was the one when dream and reality met. Theo had come through the gauntlet. His reality was his dream.

The day that Shadow visited the office, Ahanu came by with an office-warming gift. It was wrapped in the Sunday funny papers. "That trick with the rolled-up funnies really worked," said Theo as he smiled and looked down at Shadow. Theo opened the funnies to the gift. Inside them was Ahanu's celebration drum. It was deer hide stretched over a cedar rim, about two inches wide.

"We played a steady beat to Shooting Star and all the Lost Boys before they left our home. We of tradition believe in the steady beat of life. The beat unfolds every day. Every rhythm prepares a future," the medicine man said. "Every thought you have, every move you make, is like a pebble dropped into water, Theo. It continues to make ripples. That's why it is so important your rhythms be true to life's Spirit. For in that way, your future will always rest in compassion. For such is life's Spirit. It is the spirit of compassion. May this office and your cadence thrum with the kindness of your holy hands, Dr. Snow."

"I can't take this, Ahanu. It's part of your family," said Theo.

"And who are you but my family? No, my friend, for Oota Dabun and myself, the adventure in this world shall end. I am ninety-five years old. For you, the adventure is just beginning. Bang the drum, Theo. Bang it with a soulful cadence so the great road it forms is clear and solid for you and your tribe."

Shadow watched as the two men hugged. Shadow did not know why, but he was both happy and sad.

"Do you know what I said to you the first time we met? You were but a youngster?" asked the medicine man.

Theo smiled and nodded. "How could I forget?"

Ahanu looked at Theo as he held the young man's shoulders. "Say, please."

"Master the dog, and in so doing, you will master yourself," Theo answered.

The Algonquin's eyes looked warmly at Theo. Shadow felt the radiance of the look moving across his own golden fur.

It is said that at around the age of seven, a child stops seeing the world anthropomorphically. The tables and the turtles no longer tell tales.

For Theo, at least, as far as nature was concerned, he always saw the natural world with vast personality. Shadow understood much of what he said. Over the time of his many years of practice, Theo spoke to most of the animals. He looked into their eyes as he whispered to them. He cajoled them. He loved them with, yes, his mastery.

Theo Snow became the *Doctor Doolittle* of his account. The animal whisperer of New England. The animals in his care were his music. They adored him. And so, in turn, he became their song. In the night, they howled with their gratitude.

For Shadow, Theo never lost his enthusiasms. He never grew "gray" as an adult, despite all the study and sacrifice he made as a doctor. And Ahanu's drum? Theo did not hang it on a wall like the mask of the lion.

Those were some of the best times for Shadow—when he and Lora and Theo would get into the woody wagon and drive and drive until it seemed they had reached the end of the earth.

There, at the sea or in a great ravine, Theo would cut loose. He would sit on the ground and beat the tight skin of the celebration drum in pleasurable abandonment. He became as wild as wind. Shadow loved it for he was wild, too, when he received the permission to step outside the world man had made. Lora, even in her advanced stages of pregnancy, would take Shadow's paws to dance with him. And Shadow was more than happy to hop on his one good back leg as Theo banged the drum on the wide stage of the natural world.

In this way, Shadow finally understood what Lora had said many years ago when she called Shadow her "church."

Nature was the great ecclesiastical room. It held the power of divine spirit—the wind, the fragrance, the desire, the relief, the majesty of blessed existence. Shadow was merely an accolade within Nature's immense room.

Gada. Gada. Gada.

Gada. Gada. Gada.

There, by the sea or in the valley, the Snow family played and danced their great satisfaction. Their every move was prayer. So it is with one of the great truths—happiness, too, is a kind of holiness.

Chapter Eighteen

Unlike Shadow, who Theo waited to give a name to, the baby was instantly named. Her name was Emma Alice Snow. When Emma came home from the hospital, Shadow waited for the new family on the porch at Blueberry Hill. Something told him to keep his distance. He did not need to receive a command from Alice or Theo. He could see it in Theo's eyes even as he stepped out of the woody wagon.

Alice rushed out of the front door of the house. Running past Shadow, rustling his golden fur at the crown.

"That's your baby sister, Shadow," Alice said. "You'll have a new baby to raise, now. Isn't that wonderful?"

Shadow was happy for Theo, watching his beaming face as he hurried over to the passenger side and opened the door for Lora and Emma.

Lora carried the tiny bundle in a pink blanket toward the house. Even from the porch, Shadow could smell the scents of baby powder and baby oil wafting off the newborn. It was delightful. The dog breathed in deeply as if it was new dew on sleeves of grass.

Shadow sat as patiently as he did on the day of the wedding. His great mane of gold and white shone in the sun.

I am greeting a new guest now, he thought.

When Lora opened the blanket to show Shadow the little guest's face, Shadow observed the small head of the baby girl. Her eyes were green like her daddy's. Her skin was pink like her mom's.

The baby held open her palm for the dog in greeting. Human babies, too, knew the ancient language of life in this world. The dog was filled with joy, but he did not need to run around in circles and wag his tail.

I am King of Sea and Sky. Kings aren't showy. They simply are, he thought.

Emma's new room was wonderful. The stenciled animals galloped across the walls. Even the one dormer window in the room was trimmed with birds of all kinds, sparrows, larks, geese, and, at its peak, one extremely colorful parrot.

The first night of being home, it seemed to Shadow that poor Emma was all alone, even with the myriad of animals and birds to keep her company. She kept crying. Lora's concerned visits did not seem to help. She was up and down and up and down every time the baby cried.

Shadow did not have the complete answer for Emma. But he knew what had worked for him. Surprisingly, for the rest of the evening, Emma did not cry. When Lora walked in to see the baby at first light, she instantly observed the small bundle at the baby's side.

"What is this?" Lora said as she pulled it from the crib. Theo walked into the room. He heard the ticking through the rolled-up diaper.

"I know," Theo said. "It's a little gift from the sleep fairy."

Lora opened the fresh cotton diaper and found inside the alarm clock from Theo's side table.

"Your mother?" said Lora.

"It wasn't her magic that kept Emma sleeping," Theo said with a smile. "It was another's."

His eyes pulled past the crib and to the cubby by the fireplace. As he was being talked about, Shadow had no choice but to look up at Lora and Theo.

Every rhythm prepares a future.

Tick-tock–tick-tock.

Thump–thump–thump–thump.

"How did he know how to do that, and when did he do that?" she said.

"He still has a trick or two in him, don't you, sport?" Theo asked.

The cubby began to thump as it always did when Shadow was happy, his tail smacking the wooden walls and the old lambskin of the hearth cupboard.

Thump-thump-thump-thump.

Outside of a Santa's hat at Christmas, a single bow tie for a wedding, and a pilgrim's hat with a buckle for the occasional Thanksgiving, Shadow had been spared most of the indignities of "dress the dog." Theo was too busy hitting the baseball bat or driving the car to care, and Alice preferred to dress the empty canvases on her easels rather than splay it on the fur or head of their dear canine.

Shadow learned from Cleopatra that it was a common practice to perform Easter Parade for the girls in the family.

"But," Cleopatra said, glowering, "the only one in the parade is *you*."

"I am King of Sea and Sky," replied Shadow in animal-cant. He was reminding Cleopatra of what she once proclaimed. Sometimes, she forgot. She was getting old, like him. Her ribs pierced her fur.

"You may be all that, my friend," Cleopatra said, "but you will lose your throne for a while when that closet of frills opens. When hats tumble down from the shelf into a little girl's hands, there is no stopping it. You've been warned."

Following her love for Cheerios, which she and Shadow always shared, at four years old, Emma came into her second obsession. She liked to look at herself in the mirror and change outfits. There were two vanities already in the farmhouse, one owned by her grandma Alice and the other was in the possession of her mother.

For her fourth birthday, Emma received a pink wooden vanity with a pink chair, a pink bureau, and a pink mirror all to herself.

It came in a big box from Kresge's.

It rolled onto the property on the rusty flatbed truck. To little Emma, its box seemed as big as the whole wide world. Her heart wouldn't stop thumping as she opened the box and saw her forever dream unfold.

This is when the door to her bedroom closed for hours on end. But she was not alone. She had her friend, Shadow, to model with her.

Grandma and mommy owned many costumes they had

outgrown. They gave her funny old hats and even a fur stole with a red fox head on it, which Shadow barked at every time he had to wear it.

Sometimes, Shadow would be going to a fancy affair and would have to wear three white gloves on his paws.

That formal dressing did not last long. The gloves inevitably slipped off as he walked down the burgundy bath towel, also known as the red carpet.

Shadow wore a flapper hat, a hat with silk flowers, silver shoulder pads from a costume of Joan of Arc whom Alice had played in an eighth-grade performance, and even an old Dairy Queen cap that Lora had saved from those sun-kissed summers of rocket-red lips and roller skates.

Alice even made a space-suit costume for Shadow. The helmet was constructed from a cardboard box that had once held a toaster oven. It was in honor of Laika, the first dog-astronaut to orbit the world in the space race between Russia and America.

Shadow loved Emma. She was an innocent. She was a girl without a crack in her heart. He wore the space helmet. He wore the red lipstick. Largely, the lipstick was scrawled onto his old teeth, for Emma had not yet learned to color inside the lines.

Sometimes, Shadow withered at the mirror as he looked at himself with his red teeth, a bouffant of teased golden hair (the popular hair-custom of the time), and a stole of poor, dead minks about his old, majestic shoulders. *What is a king to do?* Gone was the look of the Bengal tiger. Now, he was a mere baby doll.

"You are one helluva good-looking girl," Theo said, shuddering as he walked into Emma's bedroom, adjusting his eyeglasses over his nose.

"She's not a girl, daddy, she is a wo-man," Emma replied. "She's going out on a date with a tycoon."

"And who is that?" Theo asked.

"Zeus. The boxer from down the street," Emma answered.

"I don't think that is going to work out," said Theo and then he tried to explain to his daughter.

Shadow simply glared at Theo while he laughed.

"Mommy, what is an alpha dog?"

"Why, honey?" Lora asked at the dinner table.

"'Cause daddy said that is what Shadow is," Emma replied. "And alpha dogs don't like going on dates with other alpha dogs."

In all of it, Shadow should have minded about such casual comedy, for he was old. His once striking stripes of black and gold had faded into yellow. His legs, those that were left, were arthritic. He was tired from all the years of living, and besides, the cancer that had started in his pancreas was eating away at his insides.

He had heard that term from Theo when he took him into the cool room at his office with the silver table and the white light.

"We're going to make it as comfortable as we can while he is still with us," said Theo to Lora and Alice. Theo wept in the cool room, and of course, Shadow hated it when his boy cried.

To Shadow, making himself as comfortable as he could be meant being the apple of the little girl's eye. He adored making Emma happy. He loved wearing what she wanted him to wear and hearing her giggle and get excited when she imagined what he might be wearing next! *O' boy!* While he could not understand all she had to say, he still understood all it meant when they would lay on her crocheted rug in her bedroom. She would pull a blankie over the two of them, and while they ate from a bowl of popcorn, she would whisper to him her most privately held secrets.

She would talk of castles and princesses and a woman named Scheherazade who had a thousand and one stories to tell. Shadow loved it when Emma told him her dreams. With her little warm fingers, Emma stroked his head as if he were but a puppy with all the strength of his youth yet to come, for the greatest joy in life is the conviction that we are loved in spite of ourselves. His legs may have been faded yellow but Shadow knew that he was loved by Theo's daughter.

"You're such a good boy, Shadow. Yes, you are," Emma whispered, giggling and sighing under her blanket-tent of dreams. "You are a good boy, and I love you."

Shadow would drift as he lay beneath the blanket eating his popcorn. His own dreams streamed into hers. He recalled when he was a young, nameless dog who had a boy of his own named Theo.

CHAPTER NINETEEN

As the breeze changed from autumn to winter and the sparrows, flying together as a single arrow, migrated south, Shadow heard Nature's golden flower opening, unfolding, pushing him, calling him back to her. The blood-red cardinals perched on the spare wrought iron fence of the Snow Family graveyard like ominous redcaps of goblin folklore.

In those days, Shadow walked the house with import, as these would be the final times he would sojourn through the rooms of his life. Within these hallowed walls, he honored the request of Gitche Manitou and followed the drum beats of Ahanu's worship—he had raised a child to his prime.

One evening, after he had finished carving pumpkins with Lora and Emma, Theo sat alone with his dog on the cool front porch of the farmhouse. Shadow and he settled on the top steps of the porch. Together, they looked out at the land drenched in the light of a harvest moon as yellow-bright as an egg yolk.

"What a gorgeous moon, huh, sport?" Theo said as he stroked the dog's fur.

Yippee, Shadow replied.

"You know, Shadow's not a bad name, and you were that for me. I want to thank you, boy, for everything," Theo said.

Yippee, he answered in agreement.

It is widely said that dogs do not need to live as long as humans because, somehow, they had already learned the important lesson—they already knew kindness. And as he sat on the porch, Shadow knew that Theo had grown kind all those years ago when the boy vowed at the drive-in theater that he would never hurt Lora. Now, Shadow knew it once again. He had broken the chain of violence of the men of Snow. Now, he beheld the kindness of his master while Theo stroked his furry crown. Shadow put his cold, wet nose against the boy's warm cheek.

For Shadow, the winter winds grew persuasive.

His sickness had opened like a murderous bloom within, capturing his legs, his neck, and his head in its petals. He had come into Nature's immense room, which held his final season.

But Shadow knew one thing. He could not allow himself to die in the farmhouse. *I simply cannot,* he thought. *Lil' Emma might wake up in the middle of the night.* As was her habit, she often came into the kitchen for a glass of water or a fistful of Cheerios. *She might find me there. I would be more than sleeping. My death might scare her. It would be too much for my little fashion designer.* She needed to come upon him with her daddy or her mommy. .

Shadow dreamed of one last walk to the Cockle Cove Beach. In younger days, he frolicked in the warm waves of the ocean. All it took was a "come on" from either Theo or himself. There, in the sea, he held court with the fireflies and the starfish. He wore the green robe of fine seaweed. And so, he would return to the sea. *After all, am I not her king?*

When everyone was asleep, Shadow walked through the mud room and nudged open the kitchen door to the yard. It squeaked its home-filled tune. The clouds that filled the edges of the sky were fat with a snow that would not fall. A silver cuticle moon shone through the high clouds, lighting the high sky like a magic tent

But he could have found the way to the bluff without the silver radiance. When he lay in the darkness with his mother and brothers in the Cabriolet trunk, he learned that. He could see the light woven in the gloaming. For this reason, he had never been afraid of the dark. Mother had held him in the wisdom avowed by all animals: in the darkness, life begins. The seed breaks in the dark soil. The chick cracks the sunless captivity of the egg. The pup moves from the murky birth canal to lantern light or daylight or simply the light of his mother's eyes. There was nothing of which to be afraid. The only thing to fear was the evil men did because they believed the dark cloak of night, like Ted did, covered their offenses.

As the dog lumbered down Cockle Cove to the bluff, he felt the autumn leaves trembling. The silver sky shone on the red, orange, and purple leaves, which had not yet fallen by wind or rain. There was such beauty in the branches, beauty in the exquisite dying as the leaves trembled, then fell, returning to mulch, reverting to new life while the world winter-slept. Come spring, the nourishment of the leaves would burst open through the first crocuses.

Emma and he had even talked about his departure in the playroom. She would wrap him in a clean cotton sheet and bury him amidst Alice's acorn trees. But for her to find him first—*that was not to be.* Shadow did not know exactly what Gitche Manitou had in store for him. Perhaps there was that rainbow bridge the other animals spoke of. On the far side of the tie, they would roughhouse with their kin and with the other animals until their spirits were called to further adventures. But at the very least, he, like the leaves, would return to the earth. His blood and bone and fur would rise again into the baby-green shoots of the oak.

Surely, it would be his boy who would find him. Theo would help Emma with the sheet and digging the hole in the soil. That is the way it should be—the girl helped by her daddy. Yes, the boy would find him because he always found him. Even in the rain and the wind and without his spectacles, the boy could always find his dog.

Theo would not find him weak and dead in the ignoble kitchen bed. He would find him triumphant above the grand ocean at their place beneath Red. Theo would remember him as he had once been—as the regal one who commanded the brine, who danced in the sea, ignited by the electrons of Mother Earth's powerful tides.

Shadow was Theo's dog. Shadow was his *first dog*. Of course, there would be the other dogs. But Shadow knew being his first meant something to the boy. Firsts were always remembered more precisely and completely by humans as well as dogs. Shadow knew that. Shadow understood it from the experience with his birth mother. *I have been fortunate,* he thought. *I have known many mothers. Alice and Lora and Oota Dabun, but I will always recall my first mom when I was but a Lost Boy. Of all my mothers, I will always remember my Wendy most.*

Before Shadow went to sleep, he sampled a slice of silver moon in his mouth. It tasted good, like his dreams of warm butter pouring over morning toast.

CHAPTER TWENTY

It was a drowsy Saturday morning when Theo walked down the stairs and found the dog bed in the kitchen empty. Through the window and the harsh light beams, Theo glimpsed snow falling. The skating pond at the bottom of the hill was ringed with a big bracelet of ice, the center of it soft like the inside of a caramel candy.

In the early morning, Shadow was never out long, especially in these last years. Theo knew Shadow enjoyed lying in his kitchen bed and watching the family come into the day—the talk of it and the fragrances of coffee and cream and oatmeal and whisked eggs splattering on the hot griddle. Theo knew how much those aromas meant to the dog. He would poke his nose up into the still air, sniffing, almost swooning.

Waiting at the window for Shadow, Theo watched for him to come lumbering through the snowfall. When there was no Shadow, Theo crept up the back steps of the house. He quietly tiptoed into Emma's room to see if Shadow was asleep in the hearth cupboard. A quick look told him that the dog was not in the cubby. As his mother's door was ajar, he softly opened it into her room. Shadow was not there either.

As the soft snow tumbled upon the farmhouse, Theo Snow

put on his pea coat and boots and his wool skull cap. He walked onto the summit of Blueberry Hill. It was now almost seven o'clock in the morning. Theo no longer had a misgiving about waking up his family.

Theo reached his gloved hand out to the black supper bell and yanked the gray rope. Snowflakes clung to the rope. His tugs unleashed the *clang-clang-clang* of the bell.

"Shadow!" he shouted.

Throughout the snowy wonderland, the bell carried its charm, ringing over all the land, to which, for years, the Sage-King of Sea and Sky had lifted his leg, marking his kingdom.

The snow had so covered Alice's garden that not even the gated perimeter of it could be observed. A blue jay flew low over the snowy bramble, hunting special seed. The white-breasted nuthatches hovered at the feeder. Hearing nothing in reply to the bell or his call but the echo of the muffled snowfall, Theo began to walk.

If Shadow were going to disappear, Theo thought, *he would not go to a place he did not know.*

As if hunted, a red fox scurried fast through a snowy foot path. A white-tailed yearling came out from the tall birch trees. She stared at Theo through the snowy veil, then ran off. The snow dimmed the rising sun. Everything appeared black on white, as absolute as a woodcut.

Theo passed the little yellow house where a white cat stood at the end of the drive. The cat stared knowingly out at Theo with sharp eyes, as if caught in some singular remembrance. Her glare seemed to cast a mythic tone across the snowy blanket of the world. Theo sensed her stance and gaze was for him. It was then Theo understood.

For him, this was no ordinary walk.

This was a walk in which an ending collided with a new beginning.

That was the way of Nature.

Life fades, becoming the nutrient for new life. It is like a shooting star. When it lands, it burns the soil with new minerals for growing, in the perpetually fresh design of Nature. Of course, it was more than that. That was the great mystery for Theo Snow and most of us.

For the life of us all—whether we be star or starfish—is made of four ingredients, ingredients that can be found in the recipe to Alice's hot-milk cake.

Those ingredients are earth, fire, air, and water. But as Theo walked down the snowy vein of Cockle Cove Road and into the arctic air that surrounded the sea, he sensed that fifth element, which poets and religions and pregnant women and jazz musicians point to—that fifth element of spirit.

He sensed that fifth ingredient with the cat. *Surely, she is knowing. Surely, she has a soul.* As the snowflakes dropped onto his pea coat, Theo thought that this was not only the snow descending upon the mantel of his coat, but the sacred ephemerals that he, like Ahanu and Reverend Cummings, believed ran through all living things. It was the fifth element of which the great masters—Moses, Socrates, Buddha, Jesus, Mohammed, and Big Thunder—spoke. The Sacral Spirit. *We were put on this magical planet, not to dominate and consume her, but to care for her and love her. To harrow gently. To harvest gratefully. To build reasonably.*

As Theo walked Cockle Cove, everything he looked upon had grown white. Even the empty stems of wildflowers, their petals long passed, were replaced with the icy-nugget blooms of the untouched snow. Theo understood change. He loved Nature and resigned himself to its influence. The snow does not change. The rain does not change. *We change.* Theo believed if we were truly ready for it, there was an opportunity to find a jewel in every regret. Even his father, who made him who he was, had been his terrible treasure.

As he journeyed through the expanding winter wonderland, passing the homes and farms he had known all his life, he heard the supper bell.

It clanged again and again. In the ringing, he could hear the small, devout voice of his daughter.

"Come back, Daddy," cried Lil' Emma through the muffling snowfall. "Come back."

It was not only the bell that chimed for Theo. It was also the silent presence of his dog's breathing, reverberating within him.

Theo Snow, on this day, despite his daughter's clanging bell, had to continue to the sea before he could return home. For the rhythm of the long-ago drums, even before the Algonquins, banged inside his ribcage. *My dog is somewhere in that white horizon. I need to find him.* In his mind, his dog's face loomed great. He knew he was getting closer to Shadow. He could sense his dog's lingering spirit as the snow dropped, waiting on him for one final connection before his ghost drifted off.

Theo ascended the bluff above Cockle Cove Beach. There at the summit, beyond the magnificent cedar tree named Red, lay the beach. It was the same forever-sea that held all the land of earth—where the great beast Zampano from Fellini's *La Strada* groveled, holding fists of sand as he writhed in the tides, incapable of letting his machismo go.

He understood. Even at twenty-nine, he knew the sea is the great dreamscape of all men and women. It is the beautiful and terrifying mystery of the subconscious in which we all find ourselves swimming.

Theo observed that the carpet of leaves and pine beneath Red had not yet been covered by the snow. Red's dense, rough cedar crown kept the snow aloft. The golden dog lay below the witness tree.

As Theo approached, he saw the faint brush stroke of frost at the very tips of the dog's white-gold mane. In his wide wale corduroy pants, Theo sat down next to the dog. He glimpsed Shadow's eyes closed as in sleep, his nose pressed against the trunk of the cedar tree as if he was trying to *push and push and push* the wood of the tree to some other world—the land inside this world where the spirit mixes with the microbes and the cosmos unfolds. Theo took his glove off his right hand. He caressed Shadow, who breathed ever so lightly. With his index finger and thumb, Theo plucked the bits of ice from around Shadow's faded golden face.

"Hey, didn't you think I wanted to be part of this?" asked Theo softly. "I'm your pal. Don't you know that?"

The man petted the top of the dog's crown where the splash of white fur still rose in a pale star. He stroked the pink downy pinna of his impossibly soft ears. Theo noticed the warmth of his hand melting the frost sparkling on the fur.

Even in this state, and even in the dog's strangeness, Theo could not help but notice the magnificent nobleness of the dog's head—the high brow, the royal ears, the beautiful symmetrical skull, the proud snout.

"You can't get rid of me so easily, no matter how far you walk," Theo said, almost in a whisper.

I guess you're right on that, Shadow thought.

"What kind of story would it be without me?"

I did not want you to see me like this.

"We've been to the movies. We've seen *Dumbo, Bambi,* and *Lady and the Tramp.* Remember? Don't you know all good stories end with friends riding together into the sunset?"

We're not exactly riding, are we? thought Shadow.

"Do you have pain, Shadow?"

Not much. Some. Less now, I think.

"I just wanted to be here for you, now, buddy. I did not want you to be alone. You always have me, you know?"

I know. I'm going to show you, Theo. Your work on me is not in vain.

Theo petted the whole right side of the dog's face. There was neither frost nor ice there any longer. Slowly, Shadow opened his right eye and looked at Theo. Or at least, Theo thought he saw him. And in that moment of the look, Theo watched as a pool appeared in the dog's tear duct.

"But only elephants cry," said Theo, watching. "Dogs don't cry, buddy."

Theo observed the dog blink. The movement opened the tear duct, and a single drop fell into his golden fur. Theo brought his pointer finger to the drop. He touched it. It was hot—a tear.

I'm not afraid, Theo, the eye said. *But I will miss you.*

"Don't cry, Shadow. There, there," said Theo as he, himself, wept. "I mean how am I going to help you find your way to the Rainbow Bridge if both of us are crying? I need you strong. You know, I'm not very good at directions."

You found me the night of Hurricane Sally. You do all right with directions.

"So being here with you, I just wanted to help you on your way like you'll help me one day find Heaven's gate. I mean, it's alright for you to go. I'm not here to bring you back. I'm here to walk with you. Understand, Shadow?"

I understand.

"I mean, I am not as good as guide as you, but I will help you as best I can, Shadow."

With that, Shadow closed his moist right eye to listen to Theo's directions.

"Remember our song?" Theo asked. "Don't forget it now. I'll sing for the both of us as I know it's hard for you right now. You scream. I scream. We all scream for ice cream. You scream. I scream. We all scream for ice cream. I hope there's plenty where you're going."

I hope so too.

"You were a good boy, Shadow. You were always a good boy."

I tried.

"No, you were, Shadow."

I love you, Theo.

"I love you, Shadow. I want you to go now," Theo said quietly. "You can go, Shadow. Walk with me. C'mon, I'm just ahead of you. Come on, climb away from that old body of yours. Walk with me. Do you see me? I'm just ahead of you on the beach. See? You can now run fast 'cause you have all your legs, again. Can you feel them, boy?"

I can.

"Then it's time to go. Go, Shadow. Don't walk. Run. Run fast. Run hard. Run toward the light, Shadow. Isn't that the light up ahead? Can you see it. It's just past me."

It is the light. It is a storm of light.

Shadow's heart stopped. While Theo did not observe it with his eyes, he felt the life juice leave the dog's body. In the final shudder of the death throe, Shadow gave up his ghost.

Chapter Twenty-One

Later, after he brought the woody wagon around from the farm, Theo lifted the dog into the back of the wagon to take him back to Blueberry Hill, to bury him on the property. Despite his illness, Shadow was as heavy as a sack of bricks.

"Why couldn't he have just stayed here at the farmhouse with us?" Theo asked Lora as he stood in the kitchen. "It's warm here." Lora and Emma were at the counter making breakfast.

"He was just being a good boy," Lora replied. She knew this for she, too, had raised a dog.

Theo held back his tears. He did not want to weep in front of Emma, who had looked at him strangely. He went upstairs to collect himself. He walked into their bedroom and closed the door.

He moved to the bureau. He opened the top drawer. With his right hand, he foraged past his socks, a broken wristwatch, and his mismatched cufflinks. There it was at the back right corner of the drawer—fragrant from a spilled bottle of after-shave—the small memory heap of his life. In the pile were letters from Lora when he was at college, baseball cards, and some washed-out warranties.

He pulled from the heap an old envelope, gummy from the

stickers of red-and-green elves and cartoon reindeer. Then, he shut the bureau drawer and sat down at Lora's vanity chair.

Death is a door. We walk through it with our memories. Theo pulled the picture from the gummy envelope. There it was. The first photo of his dog taken in 1946 by Dr. Cook, the first veterinarian Theo had ever admired. He ran his thumb over the rivulets of the Polaroid. Theo knew it was possible for some people to believe in the nothingness of life. He knew it was possible to believe in the nothingness of life after death. But who could ever believe in the nothingness of a dog?

Age and the to-and-fro had destroyed what had once been. Theo remembered the photograph had been caught in the rain at the marsh, streaking the black-and-white image of Shadow into rivulets. Still, Theo looked into the blankness of the smudged photo. He saw young Shadow, eyes open to the brightness of the world, held in the hands of his friend, Ahanu.

The sorrow Theo felt as he sat there was not just for his dog, but for all dogs, and for all children, including him, who had raised puppies into dogs and had experienced such early, awful goodbyes. Like all of us who have known dogs, Theo would have done anything to keep Shadow with him. To keep him young. But it is the one gift we cannot give. He began to cry.

There was a knock on the bedroom door. It was small and tentative, low on the wood of the door. He knew at once it was Emma.

"Come in," said Theo.

Emma opened the door, poking her head into the room. She walked over to her father. She stood there as he sat on the bench, wiping back his tears.

Gently, she took his hand and looked at him.

"Why, Daddy?" she asked. She still had that strange look on her face. "Why do dogs die so young? Shadow was only seventeen. He was not even as old as my babysitter."

"To teach us," he said.

"Teach us what, Daddy?"

"Compassion," he replied.

"But why, Daddy?" she asked.

"So that we might be kinder. So we might make the world kinder. They leave, but they leave us with their lesson. All great teachers do that."

"Yes," said Emma. "He was a good teacher to me too. He was also a wonderful runway model."

Her movements seemed to stutter as if she was holding something back. "What are you looking at?" she asked, finally.

He handed her the polaroid. She examined its rivulets and splotches. She put her thumb on the smudges, rubbing them. To Theo, it seemed she knew of the eyes and mouth that once had been. Then the full gravity of the circumstance fell upon her. Emma wept. She was now a girl with a crack in her heart. The sorrows of the world were now available to her. Soon, she would know their beauty.

Later in the afternoon, Theo and Ahanu dug a large hole in the soil to the family graveyard. The ground was not yet frozen as it was the early part of winter. Still, it was an arduous dig. When Reverend Cummings arrived, he volunteered to pick up a spade and help, but Theo waved him into the house.

In the kitchen, Lora served the reverend hot coffee. Alice

and Oota Dabun swapped stories. Dressed in a nun outfit from her mother's childhood, Emma assembled the bagpipes, the drum, and the bells on the harvest table. She was Theo's daughter. She too was being trained in mastery.

When the men were finished digging, Emma and Lora went to the garage. They wrapped the great body of the dog in a fresh white sheet just like Emma had promised Shadow.

"He's like a seed," said Lora with a gentle smile.

"Exactly, mommy," replied Emma. "Now he can go back to Mother Nature and grow into another tree."

It was still snowing. The blood-red cardinals had left their perch on the wrought-iron fencing of the graveyard, only to be replaced by a cheerful-looking painted bunting. She was an average-sized finch with a stubby, seed-eating bill, but her colors were stunning against the winter white—red chest, blue head, green back. She watched carefully as the mourning procession brought the body down the hill and into the graveyard.

Together, each grasping a corner of the wrapped sheet, the members of this extended family carefully lowered the seed of the dog into the freshly dug hollow.

Theo played "Amazing Grace" on the bagpipes. Shadow would have been proud. Theo had become a fine player of the chanter. Emma prayed. To the surging melody emanating from the saddle-stitched bags, the medicine man banged his drum.

Gada. Gada. Gada.

Reverend Cummings shook a bridle of sleigh bells Emma had loaned him for the occasion.

Gada. Gada. Gada.

After the song, the reverend said a blessing.

Lora, Alice, and Oota Dabun shoveled the soil over the body wrapped in white.

The women were not afraid of dirt.

They were all gardeners, after all.

Theo looked off into the snowy landscape. In the white, a tiny set of eyes moved. The eyes grew closer, like a pale portrait pulling itself out from a white frame.

A white feral thing, looking like a cat, all bones, emerged. With elegance and dignity, the cat loped through the snowfall and over to the grave. She blinked. With her electric-blue eyes, the old familiar looked out at the assembled. Theo watched as she bowed her head at the edge of the grave. Then, as if in tribute, she lifted her head skyward, stretching her neck into the white snowfall.

"Who is that?" asked Theo in bemusement.

"You know, Daddy. Cleopatra from the Turnblacers," Emma replied.

Theo was stunned. The cat he had seen earlier was regal and spirited. This cat was frail, as if, any moment, she herself might die.

Theo was struck by his dog, even in death. For while Theo was away at school or sleeping or distracted, Shadow, well, Shadow was still out there in the neighborhood, making friends.

All the forgotten beauty of his twenty-nine years poured over Theo. The beauty of such memory filled him. He watched as the white cat with the electric-blue eyes turned away. There, in front of the cat, stood the bright bridge, the tie between the immense eternities, of time before birth, of time after death. The ghosts of the yet-to-be-born and the ghosts of the dead both hovered amidst the white-breasted nuthatches poking their pecking beaks into the snow, searching for seed.

What remains? Nature remains.

The bridge gleamed—pure and soft and white and, seemingly, untroubled. Theo heard the hopeful animal-cant of the past—when, on the library porch, his dog had promised this cat that life would always be there for them. But how did Theo know such a moment? *I was not even present. Or had I been?* Theo was not only the son of Ted. He was the brother of Ahanu. He was the master and the student of Shadow. And he was the forever son of Alice. He banged the drum. He sang the song. Every rhythm prepares a future.

No longer was Theo the tourist of his youth who arrived at a land and saw with his eyes. Theo was a traveler of experience who saw with his soul. In that instant, Theo brimmed with the *there, there* of it all. That is the one thing sorrow surely does—in our pain, it reveals the deep treasures of this marred and beautiful world. And guides like Shadow do this for us—they make us travelers. They break our hearts so we can flow to the greater heart where happiness, too, becomes a sacred matter. Theo watched as the cat vanished over the tie, following the walking ghost of his dog into the vast pouring-out of the teeming, bone-white, snow-white immensities.

the dog

Credits

the dog

225

NEADS is deeply grateful to Rabbit Publishers and the authors of *the dog* for the opportunity to be part of this inspirational project.

NEADS is a 501(c)(3) non-profit organization that was established in 1976 and has trained over 1,800 Service Dog teams since its founding. NEADS is accredited by Assistance Dogs International, the internationally recognized governing body that establishes industry standards and practices. Today, NEADS offers the widest array of Service Dog programs in the industry, while still holding true to our core mission of producing Service Dogs for individuals with disabilities.

It should be clear to anyone who reads *the dog* or has a dog of their own that pets can have a powerful impact on our lives. At NEADS, we take this natural human-animal bond one step further. We bring together a community of puppy raisers, prison inmates, on-staff trainers, and others to produce a highly trained Service Dog who is then matched with someone to mitigate a specific disability. By investing in the extensive socialization and impeccable training of our dogs, identifying the type of work each dog is best suited for, truly understanding the needs of each client, and working closely with the pair once they are matched, we can ensure successful and lasting human-animal partnerships.

NEADS Service Dogs assist people with a physical disability

by picking up dropped items, turning light switches on and off, tugging doors open, barking to alert to an emergency, and pushing automatic door buttons in addition to many more tasks. Our Service Dogs also assist children with autism or other developmental disabilities. Hearing Dogs help people who are deaf or have hearing loss alerting to sounds around the home and in public, including a door knock, a smoke detector alarm, a car horn, and their name being called. NEADS dogs are also partnered with our nation's veterans as well as professionals in classroom, hospital, ministry, and courthouse settings.

We hope you enjoy reading the dog and find it as moving and heartwarming as we do.